Callie tore her lips from Drew's and pushed him away.

"Drew, will you stop, please!"

Suddenly he let her go. "Isn't that what you wanted?" he asked quietly. "What you couldn't put into words?"

She shook her head. It *was* what she'd wanted, but it wasn't. Callie stared at him. At that moment, he seemed not at all like the boy she'd known. He seemed a man, struggling, yearning, wanting something of not only her, but of himself.

"No," he answered for her. "Not quite what you were thinking of." He studied her, and his eyes seemed to change then, harden, as if purposefully. "Go on home to Mama and Daddy, little girl," he said in a tone that she'd never heard from Drew in her life. "Someday you'll find a man up to the challenge of loving you, but you've got a whole lot of growing up to do before you should even begin to play at love."

Dear Reader,

This month we're proud to present our Premiere title for 1993—it's a wonderful love story called *Still Sweet on Him,* by an exciting new author, Jodi O'Donnell.

Jodi, a native of Iowa, has written a romance from the heart, set in a place much like her own hometown. This book was also the winner of the 1992 Golden Heart Award given by the Romance Writers of America for an outstanding unpublished novel. Look for Jodi's special letter to you in the front pages of *Still Sweet on Him.*

If you enjoy this book—and we hope you do!—look for Jodi's next book, *The Farmer Takes a Wife,* coming in February 1994.

Our popular FABULOUS FATHERS series continues this month with *Mad About Maggie,* by one of your favorite authors, Pepper Adams. And don't forget to visit Duncan, Oklahoma—where love can make miracles happen—as Arlene James's THIS SIDE OF HEAVEN trilogy continues with *An Old-Fashioned Love.*

Look for more great romances this month by Maris Soule, Marcy Gray and Linda Varner. This month and every month, we're dedicated to bringing you heartwarming, exciting love stories. Your comments and suggestions are important to us. Please write and tell us about the books and authors you enjoy best.

Happy reading!

Anne Canadeo
Senior Editor
Silhouette Romance

STILL SWEET ON HIM
Jodi O'Donnell

Published by Silhouette Books New York

America's Publisher of Contemporary Romance

For my parents,
Augustine and Jacqueline O'Donnell,
my brothers and sisters (all thirteen of them),
and for the people of my hometown, Slater, Iowa.

But most of all . . . for Darrel.

SILHOUETTE BOOKS
300 East 42nd St., New York, N.Y. 10017

STILL SWEET ON HIM

Copyright © 1993 by Data Analysis & Results, Inc.

ISBN: 0-373-08969-4

First Silhouette Books printing October 1993

All the characters in this book have no existence outside the
imagination of the author and have no relation whatsoever to
anyone bearing the same name or names. They are not even
distantly inspired by any individual known or unknown to the
author, and all incidents are pure invention.

®: Trademark used under license and registered in the United States
Patent and Trademark Office and in other countries.

Printed in the U.S.A.

JODI O'DONNELL

considers herself living proof that "writing what you know" works. She grew up in Iowa but moved to California—only to marry the hometown boy she'd known since fifth grade. Written from the heart, *Still Sweet on Him* won the Romance Writers of America 1992 Golden Heart Award for Best Unpublished Traditional Romance.

Jodi and her husband, Darrel, run a successful consulting business near Dallas, Texas, with the aid of their two computer cats, ASCII and ECCDIC.

A Letter from the Author

Dear Reader,

I've always been a major-league dreamer, but even *I* never imagined winning the Romance Writers of America's Golden Heart and selling my first book, both in the same week!

Yes, I got "the news" at the opening reception of RWA's 1992 National Conference. I'll admit I don't remember much from the workshops I attended over the next few days, and I barely remember the wonderful party Silhouette threw for its "published authors." (Boy, do I like the sound of that!) But then to win the Golden Heart ... Well, with a payoff like that, do you wonder that I believe in dreams even more than before?

I'll confess, however, that I believed in them all along. It's the reason I chose to write a simple story that began in my own backyard, where most dreams take shape—those heartfelt dreams that touch us most deeply. It's also why I consider *Still Sweet on Him* more than just my story. It's yours, as well. You see, I believe that while dreams come in all shapes and sizes, our most cherished desire is the same: to love and be loved.

So, what will I go by in the future? Published author? Golden Heart winner? No, I'll stick with my old title—dreamer. But I do have a new dream: Can I make them come true for you, too?

Sincerely,

Jodi O'Donnell

Chapter One

Callie Farrell ran her hand down the dark wood on the armoire. She grasped the antique latch and turned it, opening the large door. Sticking her head inside, she sniffed blissfully. *Lined with cedar,* she thought. Perfect for her family's country inn.

Arnie Rosewood had not let her down. True to his assurances, his mother's estate sale offered numerous antiques. Callie withdrew her head and literally beamed at herself in the beveled mirror nestled in the armoire's door. She had arrived home only yesterday, and already she'd taken the first of many steps toward creating an inn such as her parents had never imagined.

Her smile grew wider even as a lump formed in her throat and tears stung her eyes. Yes, finding this armoire was a good sign. *The Farrell family's luck has officially changed.* She'd never felt more sure of it.

Now the only thing left to do was pray that she'd correctly assumed midwestern prices for antiques had remained reasonable in the six years of her absence. And, Callie thought ruefully, that the threatening slate-gray clouds on the horizon would not migrate too quickly eastward and spew chilling rain on the Friday afternoon doings of Soldier Creek, Iowa.

Eyeing the thunderheads closely, Callie was not at all confident her latter petition would be answered. After all, this was spring in Iowa. An involuntary shiver raised the hairs on her arms. In her half dozen years on the West Coast, she certainly hadn't missed the extremes of weather typified by the Midwest.

Her pensive gaze dropped as a masculine laugh drew her attention from the dismal skyline. Although she hadn't heard it in years, she knew that laugh, had known it all her life.

And then she saw him. His height made him easily visible as he stood among a group of people not twenty feet away. He said something, listened to the reply, and again the dark head tipped backward, his laughter drifting toward her.

Drew Barnett. His name resounded in her head and it seemed, as if telepathically, in his head also, for he turned at that precise moment and met her gaze. A wondering smile replaced the laughter. He excused himself from the group and started toward her.

Callie's heart began a steady thumping so forceful she felt sure her chest vibrated visibly. In the few moments it took for him to approach, she was startled by how much she remembered about him. His eyes were still blue, like bits of periwinkle at dawn. The black hair that curled on his wide forehead and waved back from his temple still looked thick and glossy. And his strong face, no longer boyish as it had been in his early twenties, still fascinated her as those with more regular features had never done.

Yes, she remembered. Half a dozen years seemed to fall away as he walked toward her, and Callie underwent a strange sensation, a feeling that no time had passed—that she was still a seventeen-year-old girl and Drew the boy she had adored.

Her emotions ran high right now, she thought in explanation of her reaction. That's all. But the truth was she hadn't expected to see him. The last she'd heard, he'd been on the staff of a veterinary hospital in Omaha, needing, like so many people, to find work where it could be had. Oh, she knew he still had family in Soldier Creek, as did she, and in the back of her mind she'd known they'd run into each other at least once during the next two months. But the chances of it happening so soon seemed improbable, even in the needle's eye of small-town Iowa, through which no one passed unnoticed.

Drew stopped in front of her. He wore a pair of well-faded jeans and a dark woven plaid shirt, its sleeves rolled back on his forearms against the unseasonably warm early April day.

He'd never looked better.

"Hello, Callie Farrell," he said in a husky baritone that soothed and disturbed at the same time. Again, his voice stirred memories, and she admitted that it would probably be decades before she'd forget throwing herself at this man. Even now she could hear him admonishing her to grow up before playing at life and love.

Dismay whisked through her at the recollection, and Callie felt her face grow hot. No, she hadn't thought to see him quite yet, but more than that, she'd not anticipated her present reaction. She wondered if he, too, was remembering the scene of their last encounter, or if he'd forgotten it, as she greatly hoped he had.

The easygoing smile on his lips spurred her to find a similar one from somewhere within, and she pasted it on her face.

"Hello, Drew," she said.

His blue eyes roved over her upturned features and oddly the smile faded a moment before being renewed and augmented with a look of fond appreciation. "You've grown up, kiddo. California must agree with you."

Callie tamped down the irritation that rose at the old nickname—more her brother Nate's diminutive for her than

Drew's. She managed a shrug and ignored the disappointment hovering in the back of her mind that he might still see her as an impulsive teenager.

"It's an absolute cakewalk compared to the constant pressure of living in fast-paced Soldier Creek," she quipped.

Drew chuckled. "Definitely breakneck around here, where shifting your toothpick from one side of your mouth to the other constitutes a busy day."

They both laughed, her tension dissipating as Callie realized how much she'd missed the good-natured joking that only those who've grown up in a small town can share.

"For a little distraction, you could always put a sign up along the blacktop saying 'Soldier Creek—next five exits,' like you did in high school," she suggested.

Drew shook his head with a wry smile. "My salad days are over, I'm afraid." A shadow of regret, very like a cloud passing over the sun, crossed his features before he smiled again. "So. Taking over starting the inn for your parents, are you? It's the talk of the county, you know. With that new dam ten miles away, and the lake and recreation area it's created, there's been a rash of strained backs from people trying to kick themselves because they didn't think of an idea like that first."

She grinned, pleased to hear folks deemed the inn a good idea. Though she thought so herself, there was always a risk with a new venture. "We don't have a patent on the concept, you know. Soldier Lake doesn't open until Memorial weekend. No reason they can't get in on the ground floor like we are."

"Oh, no doubt we'll see bait stands go up," Drew agreed. "But with Oran and Sally Farrell's interior-designer daughter from California renovating the house and getting the inn up and running, no one is likely to feel able to top such an effort."

The smile faded from Callie's face. "But my parents needed me, Drew."

His expression became contrite at her words. "I didn't mean it that way, Callie. Everyone's glad you've come back." He sank his hands into his pockets and shook his head. "It's a shame about your father's illness, especially when things were looking up for your family."

"Dad's heart attack definitely took the starch out of him. Out of all of us," she said quietly. Drew's sympathy was so characteristic of this place. She'd forgotten how people here shared their neighbors' pain as a natural role, and it touched her in a fresh and special way.

Then Callie suddenly remembered a like event in her life. She'd only been ten at the time, but she would never forget the solemn, dark-haired young man who'd stood beside his grieving mother as they buried father and husband in a corner plot of Soldier Creek's small cemetery. She'd taken it as a matter of course how much her family had helped Drew's in their time of need. But after six years away, she recognized its singularity.

"I don't think Dad realizes how long it will be before he's completely well," she went on.

"And time is not something you all have a lot of," Drew acknowledged.

"Not with the lake opening and the summer season coming up. There wasn't a doubt in anyone's mind what would have happened come spring. We all knew Dad would jump right back in, no matter what the doctor prescribed, trying to get the crop planted *and* working on turning the house into an inn."

She paused, her gaze dropping at the thought of her stubborn father, of the pain he and her mother had endured these past few months, and she wondered again how they were doing, truly, since she and Nate had moved them temporarily to Arizona and in with their father's sister. Her parents hadn't wanted to go, but no better solution had presented itself.

The whole reason the family had come up with the idea of an inn last fall was to provide her parents with more income. Although Nate still helped farm the family land, increasing operating costs cut deeply into the farm's profits. Then, with her father's heart attack in December and the bypass a few weeks later, those plans had changed. They'd had to come up with an alternative quickly.

"No, Dad couldn't have sat by and watched while Nate farmed his land and Mom restored his home."

A lock of hair blew across her cheek, and Callie brushed it away thoughtfully. "But I'm glad I'm here to do it instead. I'll love fixing up that beautiful old house for Mom and Dad. I've done it a thousand times in my mind." The worries of a few moments ago faded as Callie focused on her project. "I'm going to tear up all the carpeting and let those gorgeous wood floors shine. I'll strip the woodwork, raise the ceilings back to their original ten-foot height—"

She broke off her discourse to find Drew chuckling soundlessly. She guessed the reason for his incongruent mirth. "Nate's already told you all about it, hasn't he?" she asked, feeling foolish for rattling on so.

He shook his head and grasped her arm, giving it a squeeze for emphasis. "No, Callie. I mean, yes, he has told me some of what you'll do, but not in such detail. Or with such enthusiasm. It's just..." His voice trailed off, and she wondered at the look of regret that again crossed his features. His light grip on her arm seemed oddly intimate and sent a flood of warmth through her. "You have such a way about you, Callie. And it's been a long time since I've felt so..."

His gaze left hers and wandered briefly around their surroundings. Puzzled, Callie let her own glance follow. Furniture of indeterminate age circled them in a haphazard ring. Children dodged between the pieces, scattering laughter in their wake. A host of the farm folk who populated the area roamed about, content with the mild Friday afternoon diversion of an estate auction.

The scene was rife with impressions that Callie had had little opportunity to enjoy in over six years. Her visits home had always been filled with seeing family and friends, not contemplating the textures of an Iowa spring day, the shades and combinations of colors, the scents drifting in on a breeze that in itself was an experience. She realized she'd missed this place, and wondered why she had ever left.

Then, all too clearly, she remembered. She looked at Drew. She'd left because of him.

A sudden longing for a time that no longer existed, yet would always abide in those first fleeting moments of coming home, washed over Callie. She noticed the crinkling lines at the corners of Drew's eyes and the two deep grooves that traveled from nose to mouth. A few gray strands sprinkled the dark waves of his black hair. He looked, Callie thought, five years older than his thirty-two. He'd struggled through his own family crises and prevailed. Such experiences would naturally leave their scars. Yet she realized she preferred to think of Drew remaining forever the young man she'd idolized as a girl, though she knew that was unreasonable.

Drew turned his head and caught her staring. She blushed as deeply as a peony, then even more deeply as she became exasperated with her hot face for revealing her embarrassment. What a time to discover herself still prone to schoolgirl blushes!

"It's been a long time since what?" she asked, lighting on his unfinished sentence and hoping to distract his attention from her pinkened cheeks.

He smiled absently, one side of his wide mouth turning down ruefully. "It's been a long time since I've felt so young and so old at the same time," he said in an interpretation of her thoughts a moment before. His hand dropped from her arm. "Come on, they're starting the auction."

Callie glanced around. Sure enough, the auctioneer was gearing up to begin the bidding. Their conversation forgotten, she and Drew fell in with the crowd gathered near the back of the house.

The smaller items were brought forward and auctioned first. Callie bid on and successfully bought a few articles for the inn, things that would add to the atmosphere she hoped to create. A lidless copper kettle, she decided, would serve as a vase for spring bouquets. She acquired an antique tea set at a figure considered rock-bottom in California prices, and she began to think that perhaps she'd be able to get the armoire at a like discount. She confided as much to Drew, who'd accompanied her as she moved with the crowd from piece to piece being auctioned.

"We budgeted only so much for the few pieces of furniture we'd need to supplement Mom and Dad's own belongings," she explained in a low voice. Her experience in California had taught her not to advertise her intentions, though she doubted anyone in Soldier Creek would ever match the acquisitiveness of a pack of interior designers on a procurement mission. "The little things will add nice touches, but armoires, or some sort of cabinet or wardrobe, will be an absolute necessity."

"Armoires?" Drew said loudly, a surprised look on his face.

"Shh!" Callie cautioned, then whispered, "Yes, armoires. Like the one that's up next."

"But, Callie—"

She put a finger to her lips in warning. "We're going to need some place for guests to hang their clothes, since we'll be converting the bedroom closets to half baths," she explained in hushed tones. "And this armoire couldn't be more perfect for that."

Drew, for some reason, seemed bent on dispute. "Uh, Callie, there's something you need to know."

Callie confidently laid her hand on his arm. "Trust me, Drew. I know what I'm doing." She shook her head when he looked about to protest again. "Later. They're starting the bidding."

She held back at first to see who would be her heaviest competition. Here, she was in her element. In this case, her efforts held special significance, and she enjoyed calling upon her expertise. This was for her family, and unless she missed her mark she'd be able to pick up the armoire for a song. A glance at Drew told her he still doubted the wisdom of her effort.

Suddenly, Callie wanted badly to demonstrate to Drew Barnett her business acumen.

A young couple to her left led in eagerly, bandying the bid back and forth with an older woman on the right. When the price hit three hundred twenty-five dollars, the older woman surprisingly dropped out. The couple looked extremely relieved.

Callie hid her excitement as she fingered the red card with her number on it. The armoire was worth twice that much, wholesale. She caught the auctioneer's eye and held up her card on the first "going once."

The crowd pressed forward as a new bidder was introduced. The auctioneer grinned. When the price hit four-fifty, the young man shook his head regretfully at his wife's hopeful look. The auctioneer spent a few minutes extolling the armoire's features and exhorting the crowd for letting such a fine piece slip out of their hands. But no one else entered the bidding, and Callie began to think she would go home with the best bargain she'd gotten in ages. She felt a rush of impending success and couldn't resist shooting Drew an exultant smile.

He wasn't looking at her. Instead, he scrutinized the armoire. His arms crossed, he frowned in preoccupation.

Callie's smile drooped. Had he even noticed her performance? Pushing down her disappointment and assuming once more a mask of cool professionalism, she turned back to the auctioneer as he wound down his spiel. But a voice brought him up short.

"Four-sixty," Drew said in his rich, smoky voice.

Callie rounded on him, too astonished to keep up her pretense of cool interest. "Drew!"

He gave her an apologetic shrug. "Would you believe I've been needing something like this to round out my own furnishings?" he asked.

"But you don't know how much—" She broke off. Good Lord, if anyone else were thinking of entering the bidding, she'd have just given herself away!

"Four-sixty going once," the auctioneer intoned.

Callie swung back to him. "Four-seventy," she clipped out, turning to Drew again and giving him a quelling look. "Drew, really," she said through stiff lips.

"I tried to explain. Four-eighty, Floyd," he said, nodding to the auctioneer.

She abandoned circumspection and stared at him, feeling betrayed. "Why are you doing this, Drew?"

"You can drop out if you have to, Callie," he said.

"But I want this armoire."

"Then you'll get it." He touched her arm and pointed to Floyd. "Your bid, Callie."

"If this is some kind of joke—"

"Bid's four-eighty," the auctioneer said. "Do I hear four-ninety?"

"Oh, for heaven's—" She lifted her chin in challenge. "Four-ninety," she called out, her eyes not leaving Drew's face.

"Five hundred," he said with an approving smile.

The bid ricocheted back and forth between them. Callie kept going, even as seven hundred dollars came and went and she and Drew continued to trade possession of the armoire.

At eight hundred dollars, Callie clutched the card in her damp palm, and her eyes settled longingly on the armoire. The afternoon sun had been arrested by the chilling clouds now covering it. She glanced at Drew, puzzled by his perversity. Ten dollars more, she'd kept telling herself. Yet he had always gone ten dollars better.

The armoire was still worth the price, and had she been buying it for a client in Los Angeles she wouldn't have hesitated. And she had to have this armoire. Since she first spotted it, she'd come to believe it augured the success of her venture, almost like a good-luck charm.

She felt everyone's eyes on her, Drew's most keenly.

A cache of defiant determination spilled over in her chest. She raised her red card one more time.

The auctioneer and the crowd waited. Callie's gaze found Drew's and held. "Do you want the armoire, Callie?" he asked softly.

"You know I do."

The pause was indeterminable.

Finally, Drew turned to Floyd and shook his head.

"Sold!" the auctioneer pronounced after the usual windup. "To Callie Farrell! Hope you got a place for this thing, Callie."

"Of course," was Callie's only comment. She turned on her heel and marched to the payment table. She tried to control her disappointment in Drew—why had he acted so perversely? More importantly, though, she was disappointed in herself, for letting her pride and impulsive nature get the better of her. Though she'd gotten the armoire, she'd lost her objectivity. Six years in the city had taught her that there was no surer way to self-defeat. And she had wanted Drew to believe she was an astute businesswoman!

She felt a hand on her arm, and she knew it was Drew's. She stopped, studying the rolling clouds to avoid letting him see how foolish she felt.

"*Now* will you let me explain?" he asked.

"Please do," she said calmly.

"Arnie Rosewood told me this morning the armoire needed to go for a minimum of eight hundred to make it worth selling."

Her startled gaze whipped to his.

"His mother didn't want to put it up for auction, it'd been in the family so long. But—" he paused, as if uncertain how much of his friend's predicament he should disclose "—they needed the money, what with his mother's medical bills and the cost of the nursing home. He told Floyd he'd take half that much if he had to. When Arnie told me, though, I said I'd buy it for eight hundred."

"So why did it even go to auction?" Callie asked.

"Because I could use a big piece like that, but I don't need it. I would have told you the circumstances so you could have decided whether or not to bid on the armoire, but I didn't know until the bidding began that you were so set on having it.''

"And what if I or someone else hadn't wanted the piece so badly? How would you have driven the price up then?''

He stiffened at her reproachful tone. "I still would have written Arnie a check for eight hundred. I gave my word.'' He looked at her in exasperation. "It's still a darn good price for that piece, Callie,'' he argued.

She sighed, her annoyance evaporating. How could she have forgotten—again—the willingness with which people here cared for each other's welfare? After half a dozen years in an environment where competitiveness and ambition were nearly ennobling, she had a way to go to reeducate herself.

And since when had the ways of her home become so unnatural to her?

"I'm sorry, Drew,'' she said. "The armoire is worth the price. I know that probably better than anyone. You could have told me, though, about the scrape Arnie was in. I would have gladly helped out.''

"I tried.''

He had. Callie slanted him a wry glance. "Not very hard, you didn't.''

"Well . . . I *thought* about it awful hard,'' he drawled in a corn-pone accent that made her smile abashedly. "But you were havin' such a ball plottin' how you were gonna snatch that piece away from us hayseeds, I couldn't resist givin' you a taste of your own medicine.'' Drew grinned, taking the added years off his appearance.

"I was not plotting!'' Callie laughed, and sniffed with mock indignation. "I was simply securing the best deal for my family.''

Drew laughed approvingly and tipped her chin up with his thumb and forefinger. He held it, his touch firm but gentle. Her laughter died on her lips. Black lashes shaded his eyes, turning them a deeper blue, clear as the finest aquamarine.

"You can't imagine how it does my heart good to see you're still the same girl I used to know,'' he said. "Spontaneous, full of dreams.'' The blue eyes darkened briefly.

"Welcome back to Soldier Creek, Callie. I'm looking forward to seeing you around."

He released her chin and strode away as Callie resisted the impulse to press her fingers to the spot where his warmth still touched her. Two disappointing realizations came to her, nearly simultaneously. One was that chances were she'd not see him around.

The second was that Drew Barnett still thought of her as a girl.

Chapter Two

Callie dawdled in town far too long after the auction; evening had fallen by the time she got away. Jouncing along the gravel road in her father's dilapidated pickup truck, she noticed that the storm that had threatened all afternoon was nearly upon her. And although the farm was only a few miles away, she wasn't sure Old Blue would cooperate long enough to make it even that far.

Just then, as if her thoughts were connected to its spark plugs, the pickup gave a violent cough and coasted to a stop. No amount of cranking the starter or pumping the gas pedal brought the vehicle back to life.

"Oh, just peachy," she muttered as she climbed down from the cab and cast an uneasy eye at the horizon. She hugged her arms to her ribs. Sullen clouds moved across the sky with measurable swiftness, lightning licking their dark underbellies. And the wind! She'd almost forgotten what Iowa weather was like. But the years in California hadn't entirely obliterated the trepidation that rose in her as the storm approached. She held an unholy dread of getting caught outside in it, which had once happened when she was a little girl. The memory had faded but was not forgotten.

Callie peered up the road. She wasn't more than three quarters of a mile from her house, and although she had walked that distance before, never had it been in a thunderstorm.

She looked around for other alternatives. Not a hundred yards away she saw the warm glow of lights from a red-shingled farmhouse. The Barnett homestead. Alice Barnett would let her in to wait out the storm, but Callie balked at the prospect. She guessed that Drew would be there, staying over rather than driving the long distance to Omaha. She didn't need him witnessing her in the throes of a childhood phobia. She'd rather try to make it home on her own.

Girding up her resolve, Callie started up the road, head down, the wind thrashing around her. She had gone a scant twenty yards when a streak of lightning filled the evening sky with eerie illumination, followed shortly by the sinister rumble of thunder.

"Oh!" Callie pressed her fist to her mouth in a gesture of pure elemental fear. It was no use. Terrified of finding herself out in the storm when it began in earnest, she glanced about frantically. A fear of thunder might be childish, but she had a healthy respect for avoiding lightning in open country.

The Barnett home beckoned her, and she hurried to it.

She climbed the steps of the front porch and pounded on the door. After a few moments a light went on over her head and a face thrust itself into view through the window. Drew.

He opened the door. "Callie! What are you doing here?"

"My truck broke down, and it looks like it's going to start raining any minute." She fought to keep the quiver from her voice. "I'd walk the rest of the way home, but..." A thought struck her. "Could I get a lift?" She smiled with relief at her idea. No need to wait here until the storm had raged through the area. At home, alone, she could give in to her impulse to cower under a quilt while the thunder and lightning crashed around her, with no one the wiser.

Drew narrowed his eyes at the horizon. "Sure. Come on in while I get my keys and a jacket." The screen door, as he held it open for her, whipped from his hand and bounced on its hinges. The wind had picked up even in the few minutes they'd talked.

She pushed past him into the dark house, hoping he wouldn't detect her uneasiness. "Where's your mother?" she asked, glancing around, expecting to see Alice Barnett's cheery visage come around the corner as she spoke.

Drew frowned down at her. "You didn't hear? She moved into town last summer to be closer to her friends. And because I didn't like the idea of her being out here all alone."

She stared at him. "So you mean—?"

"I live here now."

He couldn't, she thought. Not here. Not in the house across the narrow field that bordered her parents' land.

"You live here?" she echoed inanely.

"Yes." He wore a puzzled and faintly hurt expression. "Didn't your folks tell you?"

"I guess I missed that news bulletin," Callie muttered. He must have moved back to Soldier Creek just after her annual visit last spring. And with her father's illness and the changes in her family's lives, a detail like that had been forgotten.

So now he lived in this house, a mere half mile from hers. So that's what he'd meant by seeing her around. Goodness, they could practically chat across the fence as they hung out laundry!

It was *too* close. Too much like the old days. And whatever the reason, Drew Barnett still had an effect on her that didn't need to be explored in such close proximity.

Callie realized her thoughts likely showed on her face and gave him a bright, friendly smile. "Well, so I guess that makes us neighbors. At least until I go back to California," she reminded him—and herself.

"So it does," Drew murmured.

Callie shivered suddenly, and not entirely from fright. She advanced nervously into the living room. "We'd better get going or we'll get caught in the downpour."

"Let me check the windows upstairs first," Drew said from behind her as he switched on a lamp. "I think I left one open."

As he disappeared up a wide staircase, Callie chafed her arms and glanced around, her anxiety fading slightly.

The house was not as nice as her parents', but still it had its homey features, like a big bay window with a built-in seat under it. Beautiful wood colonnades flanked the entrance from the front hall to the living room. It was a large house, for any size of family.

She wondered how difficult it had been for Drew's mother to live here, alone, as she had for so many years. Once again, Callie remembered Alice Barnett's face at her husband's funeral. And Drew's face—his brow low over eyes that seemed older even than her own father's, his mouth a grim line, the emotion behind it too intense to expose.

No, she would never forget that day, that moment when the bud of sisterly tolerance she bore for Drew Barnett had blossomed into empathetic affection and then, eventually, into a love that would grow for many years, until time and distance would cause her feelings to fade. Now, Callie felt a new wellspring of empathy that she'd not experienced in such depth before. With her own family's troubles so fresh in her heart, she better understood the hardship Drew had suffered, and at such a young age. He'd tried, for a while, to step into his father's shoes and farm, but his dreams had lain elsewhere. His mother had been forced, in the end, to sell the land that had been in their family for generations. Callie couldn't imagine how hard that must have been on Drew. No child should ever have to face such a dilemma. Not at any age. But these days, so many were.

So the acreage was gone, though Drew had managed to keep the house in the family. *Not so very different from my own situation,* Callie thought as she wandered over to the chintz-covered sofa. She winced at the combination of it and the La-Z-Boy positioned worshipfully before the large console television. The room had an incomplete look about it, with patches of unfaded wallpaper here and there, and empty corners where obviously there had once been some piece of furniture. Callie realized Drew's mother had likely taken only what she needed and left the rest for his use.

She moved toward a collage of family pictures that had remained: Drew's parents on their wedding day, the blush of their love, as applied by the photographer's brush, the only color in the faded black-and-white photograph; a casually posed photo of his father, in bib overalls, looking off into the distance from the steps of his front porch; a family portrait in which Drew looked about seventeen. Callie guessed it must have been taken shortly before his father died.

Seventeen. She tried not to think that she had been just that age when she'd believed her heart would break if Drew Barnett didn't love her.

Callie frowned and had to admit that she'd been incredibly naive then—she couldn't have known what she really wanted any more than she could have known what Drew really wanted. Perhaps if she could live it all over again, she might have realized that love comes and goes in a person's life, and one survives to love again. If she'd known that, perhaps she wouldn't have been so desperate, and his rejection of her wouldn't have hurt so badly. And maybe she'd never have left Iowa.

She turned as she heard Drew coming down the stairs. He rubbed his hands together.

"It certainly doesn't look good out." He perused her thoughtfully. "I was just sitting down to supper. If you'd like—"

"I couldn't inconvenience you," she interrupted hastily.

"It's no inconvenience. I have a T-bone in the broiler." He came to stand in front of her, a hospitable smile on his lips. "I'd be willing to share."

She gazed up at him. *No man should have eyes so blue.* She thought of sharing Drew's table with him, seeing him in his intimate surroundings, getting to know him again, on a distinctly adult level. Somehow, it seemed a much more disturbing prospect than the possibility of him still seeing her in a juvenile context.

"Thanks, Drew, but I'd like to go home." She started for the door, hoping he'd follow.

But he stopped her with his hand on her arm. His touch was so warm and complete, she felt as if someone had laid a blanket over her soul. "Callie—you seem...afraid. What is it?" Drew asked gently.

How could she tell him that it was a silly storm? *Or was it?* The sensation of warmth spread as his grasp tightened. "Nothing. I just—" She met his eyes. "Nothing."

"Then won't you stay?"

She took a deep breath, wondering at the apprehension that had nothing to do with the weather. This was Drew. Just Drew.

"All right," she said. So she'd stay. Perhaps when the storm hit, she'd surprise herself by having gotten over the worst of her phobia.

"Fine." A smile broke across his face. "Dinner is served." He headed for the dining room, and Callie tried to push aside her misgivings before following him.

She sank into a chair perpendicular to his as he stepped into the kitchen to get a place setting for her. Even with the banging sounds he made from the other room, the sudden slam of the oven door made her jump. Lord, but she was skittish, with the wind whistling eerily under the eaves, heralding the oncoming storm. She had to put it out of her mind.

The table, she noticed, had been set with a big green salad and a pitcher of iced tea. On a plate, two baked potatoes sighed with little expirations of steam. She had no doubt Drew had intended to eat them both, along with the entire steak he brought in on a platter. It all smelled heavenly.

Though starving, Callie protested as Drew cut a generous portion of the single steak, obviously for her. "Just a potato and some salad for me, really, Drew."

He raised a brow. "Don't tell me you've turned into a weed eater in California."

"No, but you go on and—" She swallowed as he forked the meat onto her plate. One thing Iowa had over the West Coast was the quality of its corn-fed beef. "It looks delicious."

"Then go ahead. Eat." He took his place and snapped open his napkin. He dug in with the gusto she was accustomed to in midwestern men.

"Oh, all right. But don't expect me to give in this easily all the time."

"Oh, I don't," he commented with a chuckle. "As I recall, you're one determined girl when you want to be."

Callie frowned. Why was she a girl to him? Feeling deflated, she mashed her potato while Drew poured the tea. They were silent for several moments as each paid proper attention to the meal. The wind seemed to have slackened a bit, though she could hear the beginning of an intermittent *rat-a-tat* of rain against the windows.

"Good?" Drew asked after a bit.

"Mmm. Very," she said, coming up for air. She dabbed her mouth with her napkin and studied the man across the table from her. Everything seemed so workaday—the two of them sitting there in the old-fashioned dining room, the typical square meal in front of them, a humidity in the air that characterized the Midwest as nothing else could. She forgot her vexation of a minute ago. Drew probably meant nothing by his choice of words. She had to remember, she was back in Iowa again. Calling an adult a boy or girl didn't carry the same connotations it did in a big city.

When Drew set his strong forearms on the edge of the table, the gesture was so prosaic, reinforcing her reasoning, she almost smiled to herself.

"Tell me why you moved back to Soldier Creek, Drew," she asked.

He leaned back in his chair. "Well, I finally got my clinic built a year ago." He slanted her a glance. "You know. I've talked about it for years, even before Dad died . . ."

His voice drifted off and Callie felt a twinge of regret. The past had intruded again.

"Does it have everything you wanted?" she prompted softly.

He looked across at her with a questioning eye, then smiled slightly. "Everything. An operating room and enough area to keep several animals for recuperation or observation." He raised a hand and gestured around him. "I bought the house from Mom, and I'm trying to find the time to fix it up a little, although you can probably tell I haven't gotten very far."

"Well, yes, I did notice a few things," she said tactfully. "It's the designer in me."

He nodded as he picked up his knife and fork again, pausing a few moments before cutting into his steak. "But that's about it. The spellbinding saga of Drew Barnett."

"I know the clinic was one of your dreams," Callie murmured. "A properly equipped surgery and the ability to care for several kinds of animals at once. I'm glad for you." She found that she was more than glad—she felt thankful. Drew deserved to have a few of his own dreams come true.

His tongue settled between his teeth and lower lip. "It's...beautiful," he said thoughtfully, and Callie had no doubt that to him it was just that. He hesitated. "Maybe I could show it to you sometime while you're here, if you like."

"I'd love it," she said warmly. She responded to the pleased smile on his face with one of her own. A few moments later they still sat smiling at each other. Callie tore her eyes from his with an effort and dug into her meal industriously. The wind had started up again with a vengeance, she noticed.

"That's it?" she said after a minute. "No hobbies, diversions?"

"Well, I did make the Soldier Creek volunteer fire department."

"Really?" She raised her eyebrows. "I'm rather impressed, Drew."

"You should be."

"I suppose you're an expert now at putting out trash fires in alleys and rescuing cats from trees."

"Of course. Notice any cat skeletons in the treetops today?"

Callie chuckled and admitted she hadn't. "And that's all?"

"Believe it or not, that's it." He chewed slowly. "This isn't California, you know."

"I didn't say it was," she said, more defensively than she meant to.

"And you?"

She shrugged. "Oh, busy all the time. I hardly have a chance to think. I love my job. Got a promotion my last review, in fact," she said proudly. "The people there are good to me."

"And no men in your life?"

Callie nearly choked on a shred of lettuce. "What a question!"

He shrugged, obviously comfortable with putting her on the spot—like a protective older brother.

"I really don't have the time," she improvised evasively.

"Really. I'd have thought by now you would have been bowled over by the typical renaissance man who seems to run rampant out there in L.A."

"I believe I'm finally past the age of being bowled over by any man," Callie countered. He *wouldn't* tease her about this subject, would he?

"And just when you're getting to the age where the game could get interesting." He shook his head with seeming regret. "I don't know though. You didn't pull any punches at seventeen. And this afternoon only proved you've a ways to go to keep all that fire under control."

She stared at him in exasperation, her face warming with embarrassment. "How did I know that sooner or later you'd bring that up!"

He leaned forward, eyes sparkling. "Bring what up? This afternoon or that evening six years ago when—"

"I know very well what I did! You don't need to give me a play-by-play of the scene." She groaned, covering her eyes with her palm and shaking her head. "I really hoped you'd forgotten."

She heard his chuckle. "I'll never forget that evening as long as I live, Callie. There I sat, in a box-size dorm room, cramming for the last final I would need to pass before achieving the distinguished degree of Doctor of Veterinary Medicine."

Her hand sank to her lap, and she opened her eyes as an acrid tone entered his voice. His gaze focused on some point in the past. "No sleep in thirty-six hours, and I knew I'd get only a few hours of rest before I'd have to put in my time at the vet hospital right before the final. And then afterward, I'd have maybe an hour to pack before driving the fifty miles home. My brain was reeling with the amount of work to do. Forty acres of beans to plant—too late by then for corn—with a tractor that'd never make it without a new set of rings."

He looked at her, and the teasing light returned to his eyes. "And just about midnight, here comes Callie Farrell knocking at my door. Drove her dad's pickup, without him knowing, the whole way. You'd graduated that evening and were still in your fancy dress—sort of a violet color, wasn't it? I remember it matched your eyes—your long auburn hair done up with little flowers in it." He raised a brow. "You certainly didn't look seventeen."

"You don't need to go on, Drew," Callie said. "I was there, remember?" Her face had grown increasingly hot during his accurate reminiscences. And the worst part was yet to come. She gave him an imploring look. "Drew, please. I was very naive."

She glanced away, distracted by the steady sound of a branch, a wire, or something being whipped against the side of the house. But she made herself look at him and say, "I never asked your forgiveness for putting you on the spot like that. It was rash and unthinking on my part, and I completely understand your reaction now." She swallowed and rushed on, "I've hated to think that was the last impression you had of me. Can't you just forget I acted so foolishly?"

His lips twitched as he considered her. His back was to the window, and a flicker of lightning backlit his black hair. "No," Drew said mildly, though his eyes were laser blue, intense.

She pushed away her plate and sat back in her chair, thoroughly annoyed. "You're worse than ever, Drew Barnett!"

"I am?" he said with some surprise.

"Yes. You and Nate—you always teased and goaded me, never thinking how much . . . how much you might hurt."

She hated herself for sounding so plaintively immature! Callie started to stand, to do anything to deliver herself from his presence and the way he so suddenly made her feel— confused, green as any teenager who'd ever mooned over a boy. And hurt. Why was she still so sensitive to his teasing?

But Drew put a hand on her arm. "Wait, Callie."

"Wait for what, Drew?" she asked with frustration. "More of your kidding?"

The first big crash of thunder surprised them both. The second took out the electricity. Callie was out of her chair instantly. "I *hate* this!" she cried, not knowing why she was on her feet or where she thought she might be going, only knowing that when she figured it out, she wanted to be standing and ready.

A noise on her left brought her around sharply, and she realized Drew was rustling around in a drawer nearby. The beam of a flashlight arced around the room, settling on her face and nearly blinding her.

"Stop it, Drew!" she demanded, her voice betraying her with a slight wobble.

He was beside her in a second. "Hey, it's just a temporary power outage."

The rain came down in sheets that beat against the house and made the windows tremble in their frames. Her whole body trembled too.

"Callie, what is it?"

"I—I can't stand w-weather like this," she stammered, feeling incredibly vulnerable, yet unable to stop her reaction.

"But—you lived in the Midwest for eighteen years!" he said incredulously. "Don't tell me you've always been afraid of storms?"

"It's nothing, really," she said with thin confidence. But a thunderclap undermined that charade. Callie gasped.

She felt Drew's arms go around her tightly then, and she clung to him despite herself.

"I feel so f-foolish," she mumbled into his shoulder.

"Don't," he said. "It's all right, I didn't know. I didn't know." His hands rubbed lightly over her back, as if the cause of her shivering might be from a chill. "Have you always been afraid of storms?"

She shook her head. Another thunderclap exploded, nearly over their heads. Callie jumped, barely stifling the cry of sheer terror that rose in her throat. "I got c-caught in one once. When I was five." She tried to banish the images that came to mind, but with the fury of the storm so real around them, she found herself plunged into the vivid memory.

"I'd been playing in the south paddock and didn't notice the c-clouds forming. I remember it got so still. I looked up, and I saw the big sycamore tree near the fence, every leaf on it m-motionless. The next second it was bent to the ground by the force of the wind.

"The dust. I couldn't breathe." Her lungs constricted as she remembered. "Then the rain started, and it was worse. I lay curled on the ground, trying to get small so the storm wouldn't bother with me, but not so s-small I'd blow away." She lifted her head and stared at her fingers imbedded in the fabric of Drew's shirtfront, her knuckles bloodless. "Dad and Nate found me there. They were frantic—they'd all been searching for me. I don't remember them carrying me to the house." A film of tears blurred her vision. She closed her eyes, concentrating on holding them in, but she felt a tear slide down her cheek in a trail of wetness.

"All right," Drew said, drawing her head against his chest again. "I understand now. It's over. Come on now, it's all right. Tell me, how did you survive thunderstorms after that?" His splendid voice was low in her ear, distracting her from her fright. "What did you do?"

"I'd get Hannah—or one of our other dogs—and grab a blanket and a f-flashlight and go down in the cellar. It wasn't so bad down there. I couldn't see the lightning, and the thunder and wind were muted."

"And is California weather different?"

She nodded, her cheek rubbing against the front of his cotton shirt. "No thunderstorms or tornadoes, but they have earthquakes now and then."

"Do they frighten you, too?"

Her trembling had begun to subside, and she tested her poise by taking a deep breath. The storm still blew mightily, but Drew's embrace calmed her. He'd consoled her as he might a frightened child, but at this moment she couldn't find it in herself to be anything but grateful.

"For some reason, they don't," she answered. "I've come to the conclusion that there's something about growing up with different kinds of experiences that either makes you feel very comfortable with them, or scares the wits out of you. I guess it just depends on the particular experience you have."

"A very wise conclusion, Callie," Drew said softly.

His quiet praise, after the humbling experience of the last fifteen minutes, seemed a balm on her bruised psyche. "I think I'm okay now," she said. She'd regained her equilibrium enough to begin feeling mortified by her actions. "I've been away from storms like these, and I didn't expect one so soon after I got here. I thought I'd avoid them altogether if I came back at this time of the year. Guess the good, old unpredictable Iowa weather took care of that notion." She tried to disentangle herself from Drew's arms, but he seemed to take no notice of her efforts.

"This one is a bit early in the season," he said. He'd set the flashlight beam up on the table beside them, and it cast a candlelike glow upon the room. "Speaking of Hannah, will she be all right?"

"I think so." Trust the vet to think of her dog. "She's still at Nate's. Besides, she loves thunderstorms. She'll run around and get thoroughly soaked before she goes under his porch and roots in the dirt long enough to get filthy, then she'll fall asleep." Callie even managed a smile. "She won't be as carefree tomorrow when Nate puts her in a tub of soapy water to wash the grime off of her. Water from the sky is much different from water in a rain barrel to Hannah."

Drew chuckled. The worst of the storm seemed to have passed, with only a light but steady drumming of rain on the roof. Callie's forearms had found their way between them, a feeble obstacle protecting her from the solid warmth of Drew's chest; and her apprehension slowly became replaced with a tension of another kind.

She lifted her eyes to his. "Well. Kind of hard to show you I'm not a kid any more when something like this happens to prove otherwise."

One corner of Drew's mouth curled upward. "I don't know why you equate spontaneity and vulnerability with youth." He shook his head. "You don't seem to let much stop you from doing what you want to do, Callie."

"No, I guess not." She shot him a wry look. "Still, I'd like you to believe I'm not the wild child who takes off at the drop of a whim any more."

"No?" Drew murmured, the level of his voice dropping as he fingered a curl of her mahogany hair. A sweet resonance went through her, making her quiver like a tuning fork. She would have stiffened at his touch had she a bone left in her body.

"Lord, but you *were* wild," he went on. "No one would have called Callie Farrell tame. You were nothing but extremes. Fire or ice, black or white, all or nothing. No gray areas. Somehow I find it hard to believe you've changed that much. Tell me you haven't," he coaxed, his voice again teasing, but with a serious note. "You're still a fire starter, aren't you, Callie?"

"Not a very pretty picture, is it?" she said with a crooked smile. But she thought of the inn, of how, no matter what, she'd make it into the best thing she'd ever done. "But I guess I am. I'm not a very willing loser," she admitted.

"No, no one is who wants something badly. I imagine you've done quite well for yourself in Los Angeles."

She thought for a moment. "It's a pretty big pond, and I'm an awfully small fish. But in a way, yes, I have. I mean, you have different levels of achievement—they come in increments, like rungs on a ladder. Failure's different there, too. There, it's quite another thing to try and fail than, say, here. I don't know why, but it doesn't seem so bad..." She fixed her eyes on the wooden buttons on his shirt, unable to look at him.

"Have you failed here, Callie?" Drew asked in a low voice.

I failed with you, Drew. How it split her inside to admit as much, even to herself. Whatever her reasons, however naive, she'd wanted him, and she hadn't got him. And though years had passed, those emotions still affected her enough now that she had to conclude what she'd felt for him had been real.

Drew sighed when she didn't answer. "I wonder," he said quietly, "how things might have been different had I listened to your pleas years ago, if I'd let you have your way. You were so young. So passionate..."

Callie stared at his mouth, just inches from hers, and a shudder surged through her. Once again she found herself plunged into a memory—a memory of the two of them together, like an explosive, in a solitary kiss not equaled by any experience since. How different their lives might have been if indeed she'd had her way in that dimly lit dormitory room. Different, but probably no better.

She curled her thoughts into herself to keep her ambivalence from tarnishing them. No matter what the past had been, whatever had happened afterward, within that kiss Callie knew she'd connected with Drew, woman to man.

And now, all she had to do was raise her chin, just so, and their lips would meet again.

She looked into his eyes, and he looked back at her with an expression that mingled speculation with misgiving, but his gaze never faltered. The moment hung, suspended, the air around them dense and motionless.

Iowa Electric chose that precise moment to restore power to the area, flooding the room in light. The illumination startled them both, and they blinked before Drew's arms loosened about her. His fingers grasped her upper arms, holding her away from him. His grip tightened briefly before his hands slid away.

"The storm's passed," he said unnecessarily.

"Yes." She turned away, afraid her face would betray her awakened doubts. Afraid it already had. "I'd like to tell you I'm ready to plunge back into that meal, but with the storm, I'm afraid my appetite's left me. I'm sorry, Drew."

"Don't worry about it."

"The least I can do is help with the dishes."

Again, he brushed off her concerns. Again, silence reigned.

She smiled wanly. "Well, I could use that lift now, if you don't mind."

Callie retreated to the living room to retrieve her purse and some of her composure. She heard Drew come in behind her and she turned, a bright smile on her face.

"Thanks for inviting me to stay for supper. I'll have to return the favor sometime while I'm here." She slung the purse strap over her shoulder nervously. "I'm getting pretty good at pies. Lemon meringue, peach, cherry..."

Her voice trailed off, and she dropped her chin, pretending to fiddle with the clasp of her handbag. The warmth of his arms still enveloped her.

She had been so blind. How could she have forgotten how this man affected her? A vulnerability grew inside her, compounded and multiplied, like millions of tiny droplets,

fogging her brain, clouding her vision. She'd have to see to
it that they didn't run into each other often, neighbors or
not. It would do her no good, and possibly some harm.

They made the short ride to her house in Drew's Bronco.
A large, solitary yard light cut a swath of warmth through
the darkness, bleaching a circle of ground and casting
shadows on the clapboard side of the house. She bade Drew
a brief thanks and ran through the wet grass to the back
door.

Her childhood home. How she looked forward to lavish-
ing her talent and love on it, happy for the opportunity to
carry her share of the responsibility that would mean so
much to her family. She loved her parents' Iowa home for
its very ability to make her feel so thoroughly the emotions
of her childhood—those deep, bred-in-the-bone feelings one
always has for memories of the heart.

But along with the good memories came the unpleasant
ones. And if they could cause her this much disquiet in one
day, Callie could imagine how hard it would be to get
through sixty more.

Chapter Three

Callie awoke the next morning with the sun in her eyes. Disoriented, she wondered how such blinding light reached her west-facing bedroom. Then she remembered she wasn't in her apartment in Los Angeles but in her girlhood bedroom in her parents' house in Iowa. She smiled to herself, squinting against the glare, and glanced around.

It was a small room, with a gabled window opposite the low single bed she lay on. White lace café curtains adorned the window, which was topped with a valance of the same lace. The walls were a pale blue against the delicate white-enameled furniture and wrought-iron bed frame. The wood floor, which could become tortuously chilly on icy Iowa mornings, was covered with large, homemade rag rugs to protect drowsy and unsuspecting feet.

It was exactly as she had left it. Even in her teens she had had the ability to arrange objects and space into a pleasant harmony, a harmony that now soothed the edges of sleep from her mind. She had never been an easy riser. It was legend in her family.

Today, though, Callie rose with fair enthusiasm, pulling a cotton shirt and a pair of jeans from a drawer and dressing quickly.

She descended the stairs into a silent kitchen. How different it would be to live in this house, even for a few months, without her parents. She could almost imagine their voices as they talked about the crops, the weather, and the day ahead of them, as they had every day of her childhood. But her footsteps across the old-fashioned linoleum created the only sounds in the empty room.

Callie reached into the cupboard for coffee and filters, anxious to add familiar scents and noises to the uncommon stillness. A few minutes after she'd opened and banged shut several cupboards, a familiar bark and whimper sounded at the back door. She smiled and hurried to fling it open, and there stood Hannah, sixty-five pounds of black Labrador and Brittany spaniel mix. The dog danced excitedly around Callie's legs and wagged a considerable hind end in lieu of a properly sweeping tail.

"Hannah!" Callie dropped to her haunches and hugged the dog gratefully, glad to have a body, any body, to talk to. "Where'd you come from? Did Nate drop you by?" she asked, ruffling the dog's silky ears.

Hannah barked affirmatively. The slam of a car door brought Callie's head up, and she saw her brother start up across the yard toward them. She waved and watched for a moment as he walked in an unhurried gait, stopping now and then to examine with expert, assessing eyes the newly plowed fields surrounding the house. Her own gaze followed his across the expansive side yard, over the black fields, then rested on the large, red-roofed farmhouse half a mile away. Drew's house.

She stood abruptly, as if the movement would shift her thoughts.

She switched her attention to the dog at her feet. "Hungry?" she asked. "Well, come on. We'll scrounge up some breakfast, what do you say?"

She'd put the coffee on to brew and was searching the cupboards when the screen door banged.

"Morning," Nate said as he took a seat at the small wooden table, his simple greeting in congruence with his personality. Her brother lived in a house a few miles down the road that had come with the small adjoining farm the family had purchased years ago. Their grandfather had lived there after retiring, and the house had become Nate's home when he'd grown old enough.

"Morning," Callie echoed, smiling at the older brother who had always puzzled her slightly. His untroubled, undemanding demeanor had always provided a distinct counterpoint to her own brash, restless personality. His hair was mahogany brown, like hers, his eyes the same violet of her own irises. She was quick to observe the sprinkling of gray along his temples, something she'd noticed the other night during the ride home from the airport, and how deep lines cut a path downward on either side of his nose to his mouth. As with Drew, the rugged midwestern climate and life-style had added character to her brother's face, the hundreds of hours in the hot Iowa sun producing similar brush strokes of maturity.

And yet, unlike Drew's, his disposition was perfectly suited to farming: constant as the seasons that governed his activities, meditative as one must be to look out on fields one has seen hundreds of times before and will many hundreds more and yet be able to see something different each time. Callie wondered if her brother ever chafed under the rustic yoke that had been fitted to his shoulders, if ever, like Drew, like herself, he dreamed of something else, something different....

It seemed an impossible concept. Not him, not Nate. Farming was more than something he had to do; it was what he wanted to do.

"Good morning," she said over her shoulder. "I noticed you stocked the refrigerator and the pantry, but where'd you hide the dog food?"

Nate took off his billed cap and slapped it against his jeaned thigh, shaking loose a sprinkling of black silt. "Lower cupboard left of the sink." He watched as Callie stooped and dragged a twenty-five-pound bag of dog chow out of the large cupboard. "I usually keep a box of biscuits on the counter. Too much trouble to fetch them every time I want to throw her one."

"Which seems to be quite often, from the looks of her," Callie said, glancing down at the blissfully content dog who'd planted her behind on Callie's shoe. "Hannah, has that soft-touch Nate been slipping you feed on the side?"

Adoring brown eyes looked up at Callie, and the stubby black tail *slap-slap-slapped* the floor.

"Well, no more. It's diet time for you, my friend." She dragged her foot from under the dog's bulk and measured a careful portion of the dog chow. She set the bowl on the floor.

Hannah scanned the half-full bowl, then eyed Callie reproachfully. Hard-hearted Callie was not moved. "When you can walk without waddling, girl, we'll talk about increasing your rations."

Nate said nothing, but Callie caught the sympathetic glance he threw in Hannah's direction. He rose and helped himself to a cup of coffee as she set about making herself an egg-and-toast breakfast, knowing her brother would have eaten hours ago, while Hannah reconciled herself to her condensed version of the meal.

"So, tell me," she asked as she sat down across from her brother, "how's the fieldwork going?"

"Nearly done chisel plowing. I haven't been able to finish those ten acres in the river bottom. And after that downpour last night, the tractor'd be bogged in two minutes today."

"It's not too much to do, is it, Nate?" she persisted. "Without Dad, I mean?"

Nate shook his head. "No. I'm busy, all right, but nothing I can't handle. John Herman's boy helps out after school. But running the farm by myself just shows me that we really need some other income if we're all three going to make a living."

Callie nodded, acknowledging Nate's opinion. Last fall, the family had explored and finally decided on the option, with the new lake and recreation area developing, of turning the farmhouse into an inn. They didn't need a gold mine, only enough money to supplement what the family earned from farming and from their small herd of feeder cattle and farrowing sows. An inn seemed the perfect solution as they reasoned that, as Oran and Sally grew older, the less labor-intensive occupation would allow them to remain active and self-supporting.

Their parents had intended to begin the renovation during the slow winter months. Callie was to have come back for two weeks in May, shortly before the opening, to help her mother finalize everything. But her father's heart attack had changed those plans.

Callie would never forget her feelings of helplessness as she, Nate, and their mother had crowded around the motionless man in a Des Moines hospital bed during those tense weeks last December. But they'd figured out another solution. Now, Callie would undertake the entire renovation, with the same Memorial Day deadline. She'd hire a proprietor to run the inn until Oran's health was out of the danger zone and he and Sally could return to Iowa—perhaps this fall. And hopefully the prospect of tending to guests with fishing and hunting on their minds would offset the temptation for their father to plunge back into farming.

Nate sipped his coffee and contemplated the contents of his cup. "It's not too late to scotch the whole idea, Callie," he said abruptly. "I could take out a loan and buy the farm outright from Mom and Dad, you know. They could take an early retirement."

"You know what Dad would say about that," Callie said, shaking her head. "He's fifty-six. Retirement's for *old* people. And the whole reason for starting an inn was to keep from assuming a large debt of any kind. I mean, Mom and Dad could've gotten a loan and bought more land to farm.

There's plenty around. But none of you need the debt, not when we've come up with a relatively low-risk way to make more money. Besides, during times like these, it's smarter to diversify our income sources.''

"You sound like some smooth-talking Californian. But I take your point." Her brother smiled. "I just feel I'd like to do something more for the folks."

She slid her palm across the table toward him, almost in appeal. "You're doing enough. You're carrying the farm by yourself."

Nate examined her, and she sensed his own misgivings stemmed from concern for her, making Callie determined to annex his time as little as possible in redecorating the house. "I'm just sorry I couldn't have come sooner," she said. "I know you've had a time of it, here by yourself since Mom and Dad left."

He lifted a shoulder. "I'm managing."

Despite his dismissal, Callie knew it had been hard for Nate, hard for all of them. She shook her head. She didn't want to think about what her family had gone through, not when everything would be, must be, all right.

"Well, thanks for taking care of the house and the stock until I could get here," she told her brother, coming back to the matters at hand. Most of the livestock had been moved to Nate's place this winter and would remain there, even when their parents returned. "Hannah, the chickens. And Pavlova. I can't wait to see her."

Nate brightened. "She sure is a pretty little mare. But particular. I must've coaxed her with every goody I could think of this past winter, and she couldn't give a hoot about me. She'll know you, though."

"You really think so?" Callie asked wistfully. "It's been ages. A whole year. She couldn't remember me, after all this time."

"I bet she will." Her brother's voice conveyed easy assurance. "You've got a way with animals, Callie. You probably should have been the veterinarian around here instead of Drew Barnett."

Callie said nothing. Instead, she stood and took her half-eaten breakfast and set it in the sink. Now why, she asked herself in exasperation, had her hunger left her, all of a sudden?

"I bought an armoire at the Rosewoods' sale yesterday," she changed the subject. "I told them you'd be by to pick it up later this week, if you would." Nate nodded briefly. "I hadn't planned to start furniture hunting so soon, but they had some great stuff. And I needed to run into town yesterday anyway and talk to Hank Peterson about doing some work. I'm also going to need a few leads on finding a stallion I can breed Pavlova to."

Her brother eyed her sharply. "When'd you come up with that notion?"

"Now, Nate," Callie said smoothly, "I know it will mean more work for you and our proprietor after I'm gone, but having a couple of horses on the farm will help draw people to the inn. If this is going to be advertised as delivering a farm experience, we need more than a few chickens and a dog, don't you think?"

"If that's the problem, I could bring over that big, old sow who's nearly ready to drop a litter, or borrow a jersey, just in case someone gets a hankering to slop a few hogs or milk a few cows."

She gave him a droll look. "That's not what I mean, and you know it."

"What I know is that you want that durned horse around no matter the expense or trouble," Nate said tolerantly.

"Well, Mom and Dad did buy her for me."

"So you'd come visit more often, you spoiled runt," he shot back with a smile, which immediately faded as she saw him realize exactly what had brought her home this time. "So you're going to breed Pavlova? You know, Drew's got a stallion," he offered. "Big roan. Maybe..." He shrugged.

Callie bent to pet Hannah, hoping to hide her reaction to that suggestion. After last night's encounter with Drew, she'd decided the less she saw of him the better. There was no reason to stir up old feelings. No reason at all.

"I'd hate to trouble him," she said blandly. "He seems to be very busy with his new clinic."

"So you've seen him?"

She gave Hannah a final pat and faced Nate. "I saw him at the auction. We . . . talked," she remarked casually. "As I said, he seems wrapped up in his own doings."

Nate frowned. "He can't be that busy."

"Oh, he can't?" She reached for the coffeepot. "And what else would he be doing, if not tending to his practice?"

"Why, lending you a hand with the house," Nate answered reasonably. "Hey, watch it," he warned suddenly when Callie sloshed hot coffee over the edge of his cup. He eyed her. "Drew didn't mention it?"

"Mention . . . what?" she asked stiffly, the pot's handle still clenched in her fist.

"Why, he volunteered to help you with the rougher work in doing the place over."

Callie turned, set the coffee on its warmer and reached automatically for the dishcloth. She folded it methodically and soaked it under the tap. Only after she'd blotted the spilled coffee did she speak. "I thought we agreed I would renovate the house and you'd help out when you could."

"I've a feeling I'm not going to be able to put in even the time I'd planned to," Nate admitted. "I'm two weeks behind right now. Drew's help will come in handy. Shoot, Callie, I thought you'd be glad for the extra hand," he said in a puzzled voice.

"But we've budgeted for outside help with the plumbing and bigger jobs. I've already spoken to Hank Peterson about it." She straightened, feeling certain that the situation would lose its distorted perspective any moment now, and she'd see it in a reasonable context.

But her heart continued to race, and all she could think about was Drew here, having a right to drop in on her, a right to wind his way into her life once again. Before yesterday, she would have taken this news with equanimity. Now though, she knew that, like a conversation with an old friend, her fascination with Drew seemed much too easily to have taken up where it had left off, within hours of seeing him, of being close to him—and while he still thought of her as a headstrong girl.

A thought struck her. "Wait a minute. You two cooked this up." She gave Nate a sharp glance. "You don't think I can do it, do you?"

"Do what?"

"Take responsibility for completely renovating this house, furnishing it and getting it up and running by myself." She set her jaw. "I don't need Drew's help. I can do it myself—" Callie broke off. She wouldn't say it again. Not when she sounded to her own ears like the child they might still perceive her to be.

"Maybe so." Nate tipped his cup up, finishing off his coffee. "Like you said, it's not like he doesn't have his own work to keep him busy. The only reason he offered was on account of the help our family gave his when they were having trouble. Thought he'd like to return the favor, after all these years."

Callie, feeling suddenly very small, stared at her brother. "He told you that?"

"Sure did." Nate rose and set his cup on the counter. "Oh, well, I guess he'll understand if you've got your mind set on doing everything yourself."

"Wait, Nate..." Callie faltered. She felt like a worm, and an inordinately uncharitable one at that. Even if Drew helped out merely to ease Nate's mind about his little sister biting off more than she could chew, Callie couldn't very well refuse Drew's aid. Not when he'd told Nate that he wanted to repay her family for what they'd provided unstintingly in the months and years after his father had passed away. In addition, she'd just been telling herself she'd not burden Nate unduly with the renovation. Accepting Drew's help would ease Nate's worry on that score.

"I'm sorry, Nate. I guess I'm feeling rather proprietary about the inn. I shouldn't, I know. Don't say anything to Drew." She swallowed, once again imagining Drew on her doorstep, Drew in her living room, Drew—oh, Lord—in her bedroom! "I—I'd welcome any assistance he can provide."

Nate scratched his head and shrugged, obviously confused by her seesawing. "Sure, Callie. Anything you say. You still don't seem too wild about the idea, but . . . It's nothing to me, of course, but I thought you'd be glad for the help, no matter what." He looked at her and a slow, comprehending smile broke out on his face. "You aren't still sweet on him, are you?"

"Sweet on him? Of course not!" she exploded, and then realized her statement implied she *had* been "sweet" on Drew at one time. What an old-fashioned expression! It suggested crushes, puppy love and the passing fancies characteristic of fickle adolescence. And yet, hadn't she just been convincing herself that what she'd felt for Drew had been nothing more than infatuation?

"I mean," she stammered, "I may have...doted on Drew at one time, but it was merely a...sisterly affection." *Now that certainly clears things up,* she thought. "I'm certain he felt nothing more than that for me." *At least that's accurate.*

Nate didn't contradict her. "Well, don't spend much time pining for ol' Drew." His smile was the crooked kind he always flashed when a little chagrined himself. "He and Maura Foster have been going around together ever since he came back to Soldier Creek. Everyone's expecting a wedding by fall."

Callie felt the blood that had suffused her face suddenly drain to her toes. Drew...and Maura Foster?

Nate fit his cap on his head. "I saw Old Blue on the road. She give out on you?"

"Yes. And right in the middle of that storm last night." She was surprised by the evenness of her voice. Drew's withdrawal last night, the look in his eyes as he held her away from him—it all made sense now. She hadn't considered that Drew would have found someone by now. Someone with whom he'd want to share his life. It seemed entirely appropriate.

"Sorry about that, Sis," Nate said. "That was a mean one. You could've waited it out at Drew's."

"I did." Her mouth was cotton, her face wooden. *I came back too late,* she thought incongruently. Too late for what? *Drew. And Maura Foster.*

Nate studied her musingly. "I see," he said. "Well, I'll go jump Blue. Why don't you use my truck for a few days while I take a look at Old Blue?"

"Sure. Need me to go along to drive your truck back?"

"Naw. I'll jump Blue, drive mine here, and walk back. It'll do Blue good to idle for a while."

"Thanks, Nate." She managed a grateful glance at him. "Going into town?"

"Uh-huh."

"Tell Hank I'll call him in a few days and we'll get started on this place."

"Will do. Oh, I almost forgot. Cora Lawsen might be giving you a call. They're getting up a committee in town to organize some kind of event this summer. You know, to try to draw in visitors from the lake. Inaville is already planning some big celebration in July, and you know it wouldn't do for Inaville to outshine Soldier Creek."

"But why would they want me on the committee?" Callie asked in surprise. "I'll only be here a few months."

"Well, the inn really is the first business being started as a result of the lake going in. They'd want some input, if possible. I think Mom, since she couldn't be here, told Cora you'd do it. And you know Cora. She probably wouldn't take no for an answer."

Callie smiled. Otie Slater might be the mayor, but Cora Lawsen ran Soldier Creek. "It makes sense. I'd be glad to participate."

Nate nodded. He was at the door when he turned. "About Pavlova—"

"I'll speak to Drew about breeding her." She was calm now. Something that had been stirring in her heart ever since she'd seen Drew again—a possibility, slumbering but suddenly receiving the nourishment that could have brought it to flower—seemed to settle back into its dormancy. The result smoothed out her emotions.

"I was just going to say, Sis, I'd be glad to bring her over tomorrow since you're so anxious to see her."

"I'd rather not, Nate. If I did, I'd want to spend every minute riding her instead of doing my work."

His gaze touched on hers and then slid to the red-topped farmhouse in the distance. "Whatever you say, kiddo."

She didn't chafe, for once, at the old nickname. Not when she craved with a sudden urgency the security of simpler, more familiar days.

Hannah was sick. At least Callie thought she was sick. She'd eaten nothing in three days, and for Hannah that was not at all normal. Every time she set out Hannah's food, the spaniel would simply sniff at it desultorily, lie down, chin on her paws, and look at Callie mournfully.

For a while Callie wondered if the dog had simply gotten into something that didn't agree with her. Finally, she decided the dog needed more than her amateur care. And getting Hannah expert attention, Callie realized, meant having Drew look at her. She wasn't anxious to face him again, not yet.

Still, one morning she found herself in the small waiting room in Drew's new clinic. Worry for Hannah and her anxiety at seeing Drew again mingled to create an uneasy heaviness in the pit of Callie's stomach. The reconciling calm that had filled her after Nate's announcement had long since fled, and she grew discouraged when the current knob of disappointment would not leave her chest. When the vet student who worked as Drew's assistant asked her to bring Hannah into an examining room, Callie did so with bare composure. She sat in the chair provided and twisted Hannah's leash around her hand, while the dog sat docilely at her feet.

Callie glanced down at her with faint reproach. "If it were any other animal but you," she muttered, "I'd let you starve to death."

She jumped when the door opened suddenly and Drew came in. "Well, hello, Callie." He smiled and nodded to her briefly while checking the clipboard in his hand.

"Hello, Drew." She leaned over and petted Hannah, studying him covertly. He wore a white lab coat over his clothes, its short sleeves revealing with stark contrast his dark-skinned, dark-haired forearms. A stethoscope hung about his neck, and he looked so handsome she imagined many a woman besides Maura Foster had had her eye on him. Callie wondered if she would be able to control the trembling in her hands, if she would be able to banish the memory of his arms about her long enough to get through this appointment.

"So Hannah's not eating?" he said without further preamble.

"No. I mean, yes," Callie answered with revealing uncertainty. She gritted her teeth for a moment, and then went on precisely, "She hasn't touched her food for three days."

"Well, let's get her up here so we can have a look at her," Drew said in his most professional manner. He lifted the dog onto the table and began to examine her. "Any other symptoms?" he asked. "Vomiting? Diarrhea?"

Callie shook her head. Her eyes followed Drew's movements as he listened to Hannah's heart, felt her abdomen, and took her temperature. "I asked Nate if he'd seen this in Hannah in the last few months, and he said she'd always eaten well for him."

"Have you changed brands of dog chow?"

"No. I give her the same thing Nate gave her. Of course, I don't pack her dish heaping full like he does. Hannah's a little overweight, you know."

"A little?" Drew paused in his examination long enough to pat Hannah's rotund body. "You're more than a little overweight, aren't you, girl?"

Hannah's response was a lackadaisical wag of her stubby tail.

Callie saw that shortage of enthusiasm that was so unlike Hannah, and her worry returned. She rose and came to stand next to the table. "Can you find anything wrong with her, Drew? I mean, she is getting up there in age. I didn't notice how white her muzzle had gotten until just yesterday."

She stroked the dog's thick fur, her head bent so he wouldn't see the sudden tears forming in her eyes. "I guess I forget she's not a young dog anymore." She thought of how much love Hannah had given her over the years, and her concern spilled over into fear. "Oh, Drew," she whispered suddenly, "what could be wrong with her?"

"Well, I have an idea, but I need to rule out a few other things first," Drew said, his compelling voice reassuring. "Come on, sit down. We'll take care of her, don't worry."

His hand closed over her arm and he gently guided her back to her chair. Callie sat, and slid a surreptitious hand over her wet eyes as Drew returned to the examining table and stood facing her.

"So tell me—what's California like?" he asked, and she realized that once again he had taken the role of the caretaker in her time of need. "I know your parents visit you there now and then, but Nate told me once was enough for him."

Callie managed a watery smile. "He said everybody stared at him like he was a dumb sod buster. I told him he was being ridiculous."

"You did?"

"Of course. People in L.A. are much too cool to stare."

He chuckled. "How reassuring. I take it your parents didn't scare off so easily?"

"No. They've been back every year since. Except—" She faltered as she remembered what had interrupted her father's and mother's plans this winter.

Silence settled in the room for a few moments, then Drew spoke. "Nate said your father's doing much better."

"I talked to him just last night." She smiled weakly. "He's certainly well enough to gripe steadily about being away from his farm." She studied Drew's framed diploma, hanging on the wall. *The distinguished degree of Doctor of Veterinary Medicine.* "They didn't want to go, you know."

"Go where?"

"To Phoenix."

"Ah, yes. Well, I imagine it was pretty hard for two people who've sat on all their stuff for the better part of thirty-five years to just up and leave it, no matter the reason."

She tore her gaze from the wall. "They didn't think Nate and I should take on the inn without them. They don't want to be a 'burden' to us." Callie felt her chin stiffen stubbornly.

"They're proud people, Callie."

Yes, she thought. Yes, they are. Their attitude exasperated her even as she recognized the respect it produced in her. "We only want to help them."

"They know that."

They both fell silent as Drew continued his examination.

"It was...awful, those days this winter," Callie murmured into the white quiet of the room, finding solace in talking to Drew like this. It seemed natural to confide in him, knowing he understood, as someone who had been through an experience nearly the same. Despite her uneasiness at being here, she felt a comforting bond stretch between them. "I spent a whole week at the hospital with Mom, never more than a few steps from Dad's bed. There was nothing to do but sit. And think. You always think about the most terrible things at times like that—what if...what if...I had to do something, so I thought up a way to go on with the inn. And in the end, it did more than pass the time."

She closed her eyes briefly, then opened them and fixed her eyes on him, stark and unguarded. "I know this inn will ease the strain on everyone. It has to. But sometimes, Drew...Sometimes I think I'll never find a way to relieve the helplessness I feel. Both Nate and I wonder if we could do more. Are we doing enough?''

His hands stilled on Hannah's silky fur. They stared at each other. Again, she remembered another time, painful, difficult to think about, impossible to forget. An overcast sky. Dark and immobile forms, like columns of stone from a different age, standing in a circle around a plot of black earth. The passing of a man before his time.

Finally, Drew spoke, his voice low and intense. "I've never told anyone this, Callie, but I resented...yes, resented is the only word to describe it. I was a kid, seventeen, and I resented having to put my schooling on hold to farm. I still resented it, later, once I was in vet school. Yet I tried to farm at the same time, too stubborn to realize how impossible it was, but unwilling to face the fact that the land would have to be sold if I couldn't work it." He stroked Hannah rhythmically, crown to haunch, his gaze fixed on his hand. "Even though I'll never regret following my vocation and becoming a veterinarian, in the back of my mind I'll always wonder if there hadn't been some way I could have held onto that land."

Again, silence fell in the room, and Callie felt the solidifying of a perception, as she had a few evenings ago in Drew's home. Drew had been younger than she was now when he'd lost his father, had had to postpone his dreams to shoulder the burden of a much older man. It would be many years before the effects of that experience would fade. If ever. Just as it would be a long time before the specter of death that had threatened her own family would completely retreat.

"But look at what you have now, Drew," she said, wanting, as her heart constricted for his pain, to draw his thoughts away from what he could not change. "A wonderful clinic, and the home your parents loved. You still have that."

"I know, Callie. I didn't tell you my feelings because I'm dissatisfied with how things have turned out. I told you for you, for what you're going through."

"I wasn't looking for answers," she said softly.

"Good, because I'm afraid I don't have them." He hesitated. "What I haven't told you is how proud I am of you. You've put your life and job in California on hold to help your parents. It couldn't have been easy to get the time away." His eyes seemed a deeper blue in this light. Deep and fathomless. She couldn't tear her gaze away from them. "You're right to help your family, Callie. But don't ever give up your dreams."

"I haven't," she promised, her heart lifting at his words of confidence. "I won't." She wasn't giving up anything. Starting the inn was one of her dreams.

Drew nodded, seemingly satisfied. He gave Hannah a light smack on her hind quarters. "I think I can make a diagnosis now."

Callie's eyes widened in alarm. "What is it?"

"Everything seems normal, and in the absence of more complete tests, which I'm not sure are even necessary—I think what you're dealing with here is a hunger strike."

"A *what?*"

Drew half sat on the edge of the examining table. "Hannah's protesting the cut in her rations. She's been used to eating as much as she likes, and I'll bet Nate was giving her little treats regularly. Hannah likes little treats. And *you,* seeing how her weight is out of hand, are not giving her little treats." He slipped an arm around the mutineer's furry neck. "She's angry with you, Callie."

Callie's mouth fell open in astonishment. Here she had been worried to death about Hannah, and all that was wrong was the dratted dog had dieter's depression! "But it's for her own good!" she protested in her own defense.

"You know that and I know that," he explained. "But Hannah, I'm afraid, does not." The sliver of a smile appeared at the corners of his mouth.

She pointedly ignored him and gave the dog a reproachful look. Hannah, in the circle of Drew's protective embrace, had the temerity to look back at Callie with defiance, as if she did indeed understand just what was being discussed.

"So," Callie asked, "what do I do? I can't let her just get fatter and fatter."

Drew stood and opened a drawer in the corner cabinet. He took out some foil pouches and coupons. "Here. These are for a dog food specially formulated for overweight dogs. And the samples are low-calorie biscuits. What you're doing is good, but start out feeding Hannah less food more often—maybe three times a day instead of once or twice. She'll think she's getting more, and she won't feel so hungry. And give her one of the biscuits every now and then. It won't hurt her, and, again, she'll think she's getting something special."

He lifted Hannah and set her on the floor at Callie's feet, pausing to scratch the spaniel behind the ears. "And see if you can exercise her now and then."

"I will." Her relief was palpable. And Drew had been so kind. *The best of neighbors.* Her earlier nervousness now seemed foolish. She had nothing to fear from seeing him. "Thank you, Drew," she said.

She stood as Drew did, and they nearly collided. Her hand went out to clutch his arm as she almost stumbled over Hannah, who rose at the tug on her leash. Drew steadied Callie with a firm grasp on her own arm. Her eyes flew to his in apology, but the words she had been about to say died on her lips. The look on his face went beyond neighborly fondness.

"You're welcome, Callie," he said, his voice that exact pitch that could drive her crazy. "I guess...that's about it."

She took a deep breath and nodded. *Leave now,* her heart told her. *Now, before you sink deeper into his eyes, before you start hoping and wishing...*

"What do I owe you?" she asked.

Drew hesitated, as if it were on the tip of his tongue to tell her nothing, nothing at all. Or everything, and that he would not take one cent less.

"I'll bill you," he finally said.

Again she nodded, holding Hannah's leash and allowing Drew to open the door for them. Outside, Callie helped the dog into the pickup and climbed in beside her. She peered out the streaked windshield as she throttled Old Blue down the main street of town, quiet even at high noon. She was halfway home before she remembered she hadn't asked Drew for a tour of his clinic.

It was an omission she regretted deeply.

Chapter Four

The weather was good the next few days, and Callie lost herself in the initial organization of remodeling the house. After her encounters with Drew, it calmed her to make lists, put things into categories and be able to expect them to stay there. Too bad she couldn't do the same with Drew.

She set herself a schedule of rising fairly early and working methodically on the things she could accomplish herself. Hank Peterson had promised to come out soon to start installing half baths in two of the bedroom closets as well as rebuild the chicken coop and repair a lot of the other things that an older place always needed. She planned to do the wallpapering, woodwork restoration, and painting herself, along with deciding the colors and themes of each of the bedrooms. With luck, she decided, Drew would have very little to help with.

Her family had prepared well for their undertaking. Her mother had several books on starting and running a bed-and-breakfast inn, pamphlets on small-business accounting and recipe books dedicated to brunch and breakfast menus, since this would be the sole meal the inn would serve its guests.

The time went by quickly as she settled into a system that allowed her to work swiftly and keep her energy up. Callie relished the time alone. Each day she worked hard; each evening she had a solitary supper in the kitchen before she sat down to relax—and think. Only then, as she wandered around the darkened rooms, did their emptiness give her a forlorn feeling, very unlike the emotions she associated with her home. Often she pictured how life had once been about that time of evening, with her mother just sitting down on the living-room sofa after finishing the supper dishes and then wondering aloud whether to fix a roast or her pork chops for tomorrow's supper. Her father would have already turned on the television and over the course of the evening would alternately address in muttered rhetoric the TV, his wife and the newspaper he held in his hand.

One evening Callie took her after-dinner coffee out on the front porch and sat on the step, Hannah at her side, to enjoy the quiet that was so different from the sounds that surrounded her apartment in Los Angeles. Her eyes shifted almost involuntarily over the scene presented to her, the flowing lines of rolling hills lending themselves to that movement. Inevitably, they settled on Drew's house and there they rested.

She had avoided thinking about him, trying to break a habit before it had a chance to become entrenched. Yet she couldn't stop herself from calling forth old memories, replaying them in her mind to see if there were a detail here or there that she had not seen before—any insight that might tell her why it was so hard for her to accept the role Drew would play in her life over the next few months. The good times the two of them had shared came pouring back over her, the carefree times before she'd grown up enough to want more from him.

But as always, one memory stood out. Callie leaned her head back against the post on the edge of the porch and closed her eyes.

* * *

As Drew had so accurately recalled, she'd come to him on
the eve of her high-school graduation, slipping away from
family and friends gathered at her parents' home in celebration. With hands shaking so badly she'd had to grip the
steering wheel with white-knuckled energy, she'd driven over
fifty miles to the city that surrounded the university Drew
attended. Her resolution had wavered dangerously as she
tried to remember the route to Drew's dormitory. She'd been
there only once, when Nate had driven Drew's mother there
and Callie had connived to go along.

She found the building with little trouble, but had to ask
for Drew's room. She closed her fingers into a sweaty fist
and knocked on the door.

Even now, Callie could recall clearly the look on Drew's
face when he saw her standing there in all her frills. His face
had been initially closed, ravaged by lack of sleep and the
pressure he was under, and unwelcoming of the disturbance. With a shadow of stubble on his cheeks and chin,
he'd looked older than twenty-five. Much older. Then he'd
recognized her, and the warming of his gaze, along with his
softly spoken "Well, hello, Callie Farrell," gave her the
ability to ask to come in.

Once there, she'd stood mute for what seemed hours as
she realized how foolish her appearance at his door must
seem. Only a few months from turning eighteen, she'd nevertheless felt every minute of seventeen or younger as Drew
leaned against the edge of his desk, palms braced on either
side of him, his expression unreadable in the dim glow of a
study lamp. He didn't seem like the boy she'd grown up
with, then. No, he seemed harder, with an edge she'd not
seen before in her friend. And a million years from seventeen.

Still, she'd raised hopeful eyes to his. "I graduated tonight, Drew," she said inanely.

One corner of his mouth turned up. "I know, kiddo.
Sorry I couldn't be there." He gestured to the mound of

books behind him. "I've got the devil of an exam tomorrow."

She blushed then, at her thoughtlessness and audacity. "Oh. I didn't think ... I'm sorry to bother you. I'll go."

She turned, glad for the out he'd given her, but he caught her hand. "No. Stay a minute." Gently, he pulled her back around. "How did you get here?"

"I drove Dad's pickup."

"Does he know?"

She shook her head, air barely reaching her lungs as she concentrated on the feel of her hand in his. *This is different,* she thought with a certain elation. Different from the affectionate squeeze of a shoulder or teasing pat on the head, the only physical contact she'd ever known from Drew.

He gave a low chuckle. "You've got a lot of guts, I'll give you that, Callie." His fingers tightened around hers as she began to pull away at his offhandedness. "So you're an old graduated lady. What's next? Nate mentioned you'd been offered a scholarship to a design school in California." He raised an eyebrow. "Just think, no more twenty-below Januaries."

She made a face. "I don't want to take it," she said, sounding sulky even to her own ears. "My counselor applied for me. I'd never have done it on my own."

"Why not?"

"California's so far away, and..." And she didn't want to leave Drew. Perhaps he wouldn't want her to leave, once he knew.

She looked up at him from under her lashes, wondering if he already knew. And now that she was grown-up, or nearly so, would he be glad?

He must have interpreted the look she gave him, for his eyes turned intense. "Why'd you come here tonight, Callie?" he asked softly.

"I—" The reasoning she'd gone through to propel her to this moment—her graduation that seemed a turning point or a rite of passage, the release from the restrictions of childhood that urged her to push on to more adult pursuits and desires—now seemed foolish and unfounded. Nothing had changed about her from yesterday to today. And yet...

She looked up at Drew and did the only thing she could think of—she laid the dilemma in his hands. Trustingly, innocently.

"I love you, Drew," she said. "I always have. I—I wanted you to know."

He didn't say a word, his face impassive. The seconds dragged on with agonizing slowness, and still Drew said nothing. In her daydreams of this moment, he had always smiled, his eyes lighting with surprise and happiness by this unexpected bit of fortune. And he'd always said, before the dream faded into a visual *and they lived happily ever after,* I love you too, Callie.

But he said nothing. Nothing. *Oh, she'd been so foolish!* Stupid and foolish. With a small sound of mortification, Callie wrenched her hand free and reeled toward the door and out of his life forever.

Once again, he caught her, large hands on her shoulders. He spun her around and she found herself within his embrace, sure he held her so tightly only to detain her. And for what? To tease her, as he so often did? She'd never minded his teasing much, glad for any attention from him, but now, after her confession, it would seem all too pointed.

She buried her face against his wide chest, too humiliated to look at him, yet, to her shame, glorying in the feel of him.

"You don't mean it," he said into her hair.

Indignation got the better of her and she brought her head up. "You think I'd drive halfway across Iowa to say something I didn't mean?"

A spark of amusement touched his eyes. "No. But I don't think you know what you're saying. I think you believe you love me, but you don't know..." His voice trailed off. "You've got a lot of growing up to do, Callie, and life will catch up to you all too soon. Be glad you can gather that maturity over the next few years, instead of having it thrust on you." He cocked his head to one side, examining her. "You're just starting out, Callie. Don't you wonder about all the possibilities and opportunities you have waiting for you?"

"Of course I wonder what's out there. What ... different places are like. How I would manage on my own." She turned her eyes up to meet his, wetting her lips. "But I want you, more than anything."

He groaned softly, his arms tightening about her. "Oh, Callie," Drew said quietly and sighed. "I know you don't want to hear this right now. But you're still so young. You shouldn't limit your dreams on a whim."

"You think ... you think what I feel for you is a *whim?*" she choked.

His hand curled around the back of her neck, under her hair, and squeezed. "I think you'll always have it in you to get whatever you want, and right now you just think that's something to do with me."

"And what about how I *feel?*" she demanded desperately.

"What about how you feel?" His hand slid around and caught her pointed chin, held it so his eyes could fully search hers. "Tell me."

"I did tell you!"

"No—tell me. Tell me what you mean when you say you want me, more than anything."

She struggled with her thoughts. "I wish you would...that we were—" Visions that had played at the edge of her mind for the last several months sprang into her head. Visions of Drew caring for her, sharing with her, loving her as she so wanted him to... But she could find no voice for those emotions, barely having a grip on them herself.

"I don't know what I want," she admitted in a whisper, willing him to look into her eyes and see how she felt without her having to tell him. He stared back at her and, bless him, she could see him trying. Trying—and, it seemed, failing.

Her heart sank. Couldn't he see she didn't want to live without him? But could he live without her? She looked into those blue eyes and wanted to believe that he couldn't. Yet he was urging her to search for another future, without him.

He didn't love her, had never given her a reason to think he might. It had all been in her mind. She'd believed it because she'd wanted so badly for it to be so.

Tears sprang to her eyes, despite herself. Her mouth trembled, and Drew's gaze dropped to it. "I'm sorry, Drew."

"Sorry?"

"For bothering you. For..." *For loving you, if this is what love feels like.*

"Please, Callie, don't be sorry," he whispered. Then, with his hand on her chin, he lifted her head higher to accommodate the descent of his mouth to hers.

Oh, it was sweet! All the more so for its unexpectedness. Dazed by this turn of events, she trembled again, and his arm brought her closer, stilling her shivering, warming her against his solid length. His mouth was gently persistent, and she obliged him by opening slowly, not wanting either her inexperience or intense reaction to his touch to disturb this moment. The touching that came then, more intimate than she'd ever known, open mouths sealed together, was electric to her unsophisticated senses.

Her hands crept crablike up his chest, clenching and unclenching, until they reached the column of his neck. She touched his heated flesh with the flat of her palms and, to her surprise, that innocent contact made Drew groan.

"Oh, Callie, Callie," he murmured against her cheek, "I could lose myself in you. So easily." His lips found hers again, and she felt him try to do just that. His arm shook as it brought her closer still, his hand cupped the back of her head and guided its angle so he could find her sweetness more completely, more deeply.

Desperate. He seemed...desperate, with a frustration that seemed to reach out to her, into her. His caresses became rougher, more needful. And with a start, Callie knew she hadn't the strength or knowledge to meet and ease that frustration or desire. His need seized her and held her and asked her to respond. It wasn't quite right, this need, she thought through a haze of sensation. But more than that, it was beyond her experience, and unless they stopped now she would fail him. She would shame herself—and him—to let this continue.

She tore her lips from his, pushing at his chest insistently and then more frantically when he did not release her immediately. "Drew, stop!" She heard her voice, much too thin, almost a wail. "Will you stop, please!"

Suddenly he let her go, and she stumbled back against the door. His pupils were dilated, large and black. "Isn't that what you wanted?" he asked—quietly, though she could see his chest rise and fall with the depth of his breathing. "What you couldn't put into words?"

She shook her head dumbly. It *was* what she'd wanted, but it wasn't. Callie stared at him. At that moment, he seemed not at all like the boy she'd known. He seemed a man, struggling, yearning, wanting something of not only her but of himself.

"No," he answered for her. "Not quite what you were thinking of." He studied her, and his eyes seemed to change then, harden, as if purposefully. "Go on home to Mama and Daddy, little girl," he said in a tone that she'd never heard from Drew in her life. "Go on." He smiled, not quite the old teasing smile she'd always known, but almost. "Someday, you'll find a man up to the challenge of loving you, but you've got a whole lot of growing up to do before you should even begin to play at love."

The shock of it, the intensity of his touch, then the harshness, then the teasing, which would never, ever sound the same to her ears after this night, was too much for Callie. She tried to think of a scathing epithet to hurl at him, something to save face and get her out of there.

"Go to hell, Drew Barnett," she said, realizing immediately that the very triteness of her profanity demonstrated just how innocent she really was. She searched for the doorknob behind her, grasped it and turned, and then she was out of that dark, closed-in room, running down the brightly lit hallway, tears blurring her sight.

Callie opened her eyes. The sun had nearly set as she had sat in thought. Until today, she'd pondered the meaning of the words Drew spoke in that split second before the door slammed behind her.

Hell? Too late, kiddo. I've been there.

Now she knew what he meant.

Shifting forward restlessly, she turned to examine the Iowa countryside. It was a view bounded by her experience, her perspective that was grounded, always seen from the same level. But from her position of looking back on that night six years ago, Callie finally realized what she *had* wanted from Drew: She'd wanted him to tell her everything would be all right, that life would be a tidy affair with no unfinished seams, where wanting was enough to make anything so.

Drew had not given her that assurance. Not then, and not the other day as they'd stared into each other's eyes in his examining room. No, he too didn't know how to salve a restless soul as it struggled through life.

With a small sound, Callie looked up, and the ache that filled her seemed as big as the night sky.

Callie was digging weeds along the gravel road a few days later when Drew drove by. She answered the nod of his head with a curt one of her own, hoping he would continue on down the road, but his Bronco crunched to a stop beside her.

She realized dismally what she must look like. Her hair was pulled back in a braid and perspiration trickled down her brow. A few wisps of hair clung wetly to her neck, and she didn't have a speck of makeup on. A large muddy spot where she had knelt on the still soggy ground pasted a patch of denim to her knee, and large damp crescents grew under the arms of her shirt.

She continued hacking nonchalantly at a particularly healthy dandelion as Drew got out of his truck, slamming the door behind him.

"There's a herbicide spray that can take care of those things without all the work, you know," he commented to her bent head. Hannah abandoned her post under the large buckeye tree in the front yard to come inspect the visitor.

Callie straightened and leaned back on her hoe, squinting up at him. "I need the exercise," she said with sarcasm, to cover her irritation at being discovered in such a state.

He nodded in agreement. "I guess the sedentary life around here could pose a threat to one's figure." He smiled innocently, and she gave him a sardonic look. "You could pitch manure over at Anderson's hog complex if you really want a workout. They're looking for help right now. Hey there, Hannah." He squatted and rumpled the dog's curly black coat.

"Thanks, no," Callie answered, studying him as he scratched Hannah with a practiced hand. *He* certainly wasn't hard on the eyes today. He wore the same snug, faded jeans as he had last week, or a pair very much like them, and he had on a light blue chambray work shirt that made his eyes stand out on his face like blue stars.

Drew's eyes shifted from Hannah to an area at Callie's knees and continued upward. She knew he was taking in her dishabille, and she could have kicked herself for not spending more time on her grooming that morning. But two of the chickens had escaped from the old coop—which had pleased Hannah immensely, though not Callie. Then, after she'd corralled the errant birds, she'd no sooner stepped into the house than she saw a mouse treading across her kitchen counter. She'd run into town for mousetraps and spent an hour divining just where a mouse might trek in its quest for food, and placed traps along that route. By that time she'd decided to get going on the weeds out front while the sun shone.

"How's Hannah doing?" Drew asked, his eyes focused on her cheek. He made a motion with his finger on his own cheek, and she stared at him, puzzled for a few seconds before her hand went to her face and came away with a dollop of mud.

She looked at the mud and then around her before she shrugged and wiped her hand on the seat of her jeans. "Fine. We still have an occasional stare-down at suppertime, but I think she realizes I'm on to her game—and she doesn't have any room to be choosy, since I *am* the only game in town."

"Good. And the renovating?"

"Fine, too. I've been stripping wallpaper, but I decided to take a break today and I'm using the time to more or less try to get the yard in shape and plant a garden before it's too late."

He grabbed a handful of fur at the back of Hannah's neck and shook it as the dog groaned in ecstasy. "Need any help?"

"I've got plenty, thanks," Callie answered. If she started accepting the odd offer from him, sure as anything he'd start dropping by whenever the urge struck him. And she intended to demonstrate as much as possible that his help, though welcome, need only be cursory. "Hank Peterson is set to do the floors, carpentry and plumbing for me, and I have a handle on the other stuff." She pulled herself to her full height. Even if she looked like a ragamuffin, she could still try to convey an air of competence. "I know you've offered to lend me a hand, Drew, and I appreciate it, believe me. But really, there's nothing I can't manage."

Drew said nothing, still crouched before her, but frowned at her tone. He stood to leave. "I see. Well, nice to chat with you."

She watched as he turned and started for the Bronco, telling herself that that was what she had been trying to get him to do since he had driven up. But she hadn't needed to sound so ungrateful.

"Uh, wait, Drew," Callie said.

He stopped, his hand on the door handle, and raised a black brow. "Yes?"

She shifted the hoe from one hand to the other. She'd talked to several people in town about breeding Pavlova, and all of them had recommended talking to Drew. She was reluctant to prolong her contact with him, but if there was a chance of breeding the mare, Callie couldn't put it off much longer. As it was, Pavlova wouldn't foal until next spring, even if she conceived right away. Callie pushed down the lump of disappointment that rose in her when she thought of a tiny foal being born when she wasn't there.

"Well, I *could* use some advice, if you don't mind," she said reconcilingly.

Drew walked back over. "Shoot."

"I'm thinking of breeding Pavlova, and, well, since you're the vet in this area, I thought you'd know how I might do it."

Now both his eyebrows shot up suggestively. "Oh, I definitely know *how*. The question is when and where."

Callie blushed. He seemed unable to carry on a conversation without baiting her at least once. "And how much," she retorted. "I heard you had a new stallion you might be able to, you know...um, rent me, or something."

Drew set his hands on his hips and regarded her with his sky blue scrutiny. "And what did Nate say to your suggestion?"

"Well, Nate wasn't exactly for the idea, but I've been thinking about it for some time now—" She broke off. Why on earth was she explaining? "She's my horse. I can breed her if I want to."

"Nate's been caring for her for the past six months, hasn't he?" Drew asked, and widened his eyes at her, as if seeking clarification of his point.

Both he and Nate seemed determined to remind her constantly of their part in this matter. Callie's chin jutted out as she lifted it stubbornly. "Look, do you want to discuss this or not?"

"I'm game." Drew surveyed her thoughtfully. "Sancho's got all the qualifications. In fact, he's got the finest bloodlines in these parts. I got him from a quarter-horse ranch. In Texas, he used to bring in quite a fee for covering a mare.''

"Like how much?''

Drew named a figure that made her gasp.

"Well,'' she protested, "I certainly don't need champion bloodlines just to produce a healthy, sturdy foal. Maybe I could find someone else with a stallion I could hire.''

"Not much call for that sort of service around here. But let me see.'' Drew squinted skyward in thought. "I heard Bob Tanner had a stallion.''

"Bob Tanner?'' she repeated weakly.

"Yeah. You remember Bob. He doesn't have that still any more. Sheriff made him tear it down. He does have a patch of weeds out back he tends pretty solicitously, though.'' He appeared more hopeful than she felt. "You might try him. What they say about him isn't true, you know. Most of it, anyway.''

"There's no one else?''

Drew shook his head. "Could be. But I'd probably know if there was, and I can't think of anyone right now. People aren't much interested in keeping horses anymore. They'd rather put their money into other things.''

She shot him a rueful look. "Like armoires, I dare say.'' She nestled her chin into the circle created by her thumb and fingers as they gripped the top of the hoe. Maybe she'd have to wait till next year to breed Pavlova. She knew right now she didn't have even half the amount Drew had named to spend on stud fees. And as for Bob Tanner, Callie shivered. With her luck, she would be there when the sheriff happened to discover Bob's little patch of "weeds.''

She frowned dejectedly and whacked at a thistle half-heartedly with the square blade. "Well...'' she finally sighed. "I guess that's that.''

"What's what?''

She looked up at him and turned a hand palm up between them. "I don't have the money to rent Sancho, and if there's not another stallion in the area I'm out of luck, don't you think?'' She let her arm drop to her side.

"Did I say I'd charge you to use Sancho's considerable talents?"

She searched back over their conversation. "No, but—"

"Really, Callie, you've developed quite a habit of jumping to conclusions."

Her spirits rose. "You mean you'd let me have Sancho for nothing?" She felt excitement balloon in her for just seconds before she deflated it with a quelling thought. "I couldn't do that, Drew," she said regretfully, her glance dropping. "I mean, renting Sancho for stud fees is part of your livelihood. It wouldn't be right to take advantage of your generosity."

"Why wouldn't it be right? After all, he's my horse," he said, echoing her earlier words.

She felt her face flush as she realized how she must have sounded. Then a thought struck her. "Maybe we could come up with some other form of payment."

"Oh? And what are the alternatives?" he asked in an absolutely provocative manner.

Callie closed her eyes in order to concentrate on admonishing the thousands of cells in her body that had stood up and volunteered for his suggestion. She swallowed and opened her eyes, not looking at him. "I don't know. I—I could help you renovate your own house."

"It would seem you have your hands full with redoing this place. I want to help lessen the work to do, not add to it."

Callie said nothing. And what she wanted, she thought but couldn't say, was to prevent encounters like this with Drew. She had to stop seeing him—running into him, talking to him. She had a sudden premonition she'd find herself depending on him for more than just to get a job done. But how was she to convey her appreciation for his assistance while gently refusing it?

"You're right," she said, deciding to eliminate one avenue of assistance, at least. "Feeding and tending a foal would only add to Nate's responsibilities. When I mentioned the matter to him, he had much the same reaction as you."

Drew frowned. "That isn't what I meant, Callie—"

"No." She held up a hand, smiling ruefully. "I wasn't thinking of anything but my own wants and wishes. Forget I ever mentioned Pavlova."

He looked ready to protest for a moment. He studied her intently, and she wondered if he discerned her real reasons for dropping the subject.

"If that's what you really do want, Callie," he finally said. She nodded, avoiding his eyes, and watched him climb into his Bronco and continue on down the road.

It wasn't what she really wanted, but she was learning how to do without. And she was getting quite good at dealing with disappointment.

Chapter Five

Callie struggled to hold the heavy antiquated steamer head against the patch of wallpaper. Just a few more minutes, she told her nose, which was itching to beat the band. Probably the last ten drops of perspiration had finally gotten to the poor thing. She wiggled her nose, stuck her bottom lip out and blew on it, but nothing helped. It still itched.

"What are you doing?"

She jumped and looked over her shoulder at the frowning Drew who stood in the doorway of the living room. She'd been concentrating so hard on her itchy nose she hadn't even heard him come in.

"The Prince of Wales and I are having tea," she said flippantly. This was exactly the situation she'd hoped to avoid—Drew dropping by with no notice, catching her off guard. "What are you doing here?"

He strode across the room to relieve her of the steamer head. "Nate had a feeling you'd try something like this. He couldn't make it over so he asked me to check on you. Good thing I did, too. It's hotter'n an oven in here. You'd have passed out from heat exhaustion in another hour, I'd wager."

Only the fact that she was vigorously scratching her nose prevented Callie from interrupting his little scolding, but now she let fire. "It boggles my small mind why the two of you don't just let me die and relieve yourselves of the distasteful burden of saving me from my own folly."

He glanced down at her tolerantly, holding the steamer head in place with seemingly little effort. "Very funny." He surveyed her. "Take a break, okay? How about a glass of iced tea?"

"Coming right up," she obliged, noting with satisfaction that a thin, damp wedge of material had already imprinted itself between his shoulder blades. Let him sweat it for a while if he wanted to help so darned badly.

She took her sweet time mixing up the tea, and once in the cool kitchen realized that, indeed, it was incredibly hot in the living room. She splashed her face and the back of her neck with cold water and it felt heavenly. She didn't need a mirror to tell her that once again she looked and smelled like a farmhand, Drew's cue to turn up. Her T-shirt was plastered to her, and the waistband of her shorts was dark with sweat. If only her L.A. friends could see her now.

Her blithe sail into the living room a few minutes later, tray in hand, was arrested by the sight of Drew, shirtless, the strong muscles of his back straining as he held the steamer head to the wall. He must have heard her come in, for he glanced over his shoulder.

"Good God, how do you do this by yourself?"

She stood rooted to the floor and her throat worked nervously. "Very slowly," she finally croaked. "I hold the head and steam patches of the paper till I get tired, and scrape them off in between. I don't go at it like a zealot, you know. I take a lot of breaks."

"Well, ah," he worked his mouth back and forth in a motion familiar to Callie, "could you do me a favor and scratch my nose?"

She set down the tray and approached him with thinly disguised misgiving. *Concentrate, girl. It's just Drew.* Tentatively, she crooked an index finger and reached over the slick, bulging bicep at eye level to apply her short nail to the bridge of his nose. "Here?"

"There. Ah, that's it. Thanks." He looked down at her and laughed.

"What's so funny?"

"Your face, all screwed up like that. I know I'm not particularly savory right now, but neither are you, darlin'."

Little zings of emotion fanned out along her extremities like explosions on a string of firecrackers. Why'd he have to do that? Laugh like that, call her darlin', make her forget she didn't want him here, so close, so accessible?

She glanced at the tray. "Tea's ready, Your Highness," she joked.

"Great." He hefted the steamer head to the floor and she helped him peel the damp patch of flowered paper from the wall.

"It'll be cooler on the porch," she suggested as she picked up the tray, not thinking until she was out there about the dearth of seats.

She set the tea down on a small table and opted for settling against the porch rail, instead of next to Drew on the more intimate porch swing. He'd slipped his shirt on but it hung open, revealing the sprinkling of dark hair on his chest. Callie grasped the slick tea glass in both hands to keep from dropping it.

"Honestly," Drew pulled a bandanna from his hip pocket and ran it over his face, "I don't think even with breaks you ought to be doing that work by yourself."

She took a sip of tea to keep a defensively tart remark from slipping out. "The living room's the last that needs paper stripped, so I won't be subjected to the sweat bath much longer."

"Why not wait until this warm spell passes?"

"Really, Drew." She pinched the collar of her T-shirt with two fingers and pulled it away from her chest. "The weather's only going to get hotter." She looked at him earnestly. "Will you—and Nate—just trust me to use my best judgment on this?"

He studied her for a moment, then nodded. "Sure." He took a hearty gulp of tea. "When's Hank expected to do the rest of the stuff?"

"He's coming out tomorrow to start on the bedroom closets that'll be converted to half baths. That's the most extensive change needed."

"Really," he said with a thoughtful quirk of his mouth. "And what else does one do to turn a regular old farmhouse into a country inn?"

"Well, mostly it's restoring the house as much as possible to its authentic motif and adding antique furniture, like high beds with colorful quilts, and hanging muslin curtains at the windows. You want to create a real homey atmosphere." She placed the cool glass of tea against her cheek speculatively. "I haven't really decided on the final details of the bedrooms. I'm tempted to let them take shape on their own, just as one would expect in a farm home. You know, bric-a-brac here and there, old photos in quaint frames. Everything needn't match, as long as it presents a unified feeling."

"How many rooms will you have for guests?" Drew asked.

"Four," she said, warming to her subject. "Mom and Dad's, Nate's, the spare bedroom and the room Mom used for sewing. The den and family room off the kitchen will be outfitted as the proprietor's living quarters."

"The proprietor?"

Callie nodded. "I'm hoping I'll find someone, maybe an older woman, who's looking for some extra money, just through the summer. The place really won't take much upkeep. Just a few hours in the morning straightening rooms and making breakfast." She concentrated on the toe of her shoe, thinking about Pavlova. Even without a foal, the mare would be a responsibility. "Well, maybe a little more time than that. But we want someone who doesn't need something permanent. Mom and Dad will be back in the fall."

Drew leaned forward, propping his elbows on his knees. "You didn't mention your bedroom. What's it to be used for?"

"We'd thought about using it for storage—linens, cleaning supplies." She shook her head and raised her glass to her lips. "But I'm thinking, why not rent it out too? It's small, but it's the only room that I would barely need to touch, so far as decorating it."

"Really?"

"Oh, yes. It's already done in antique lace and white wrought iron. I did it when I was in high school," she said proudly. "You should see it."

"I can only imagine," Drew said with a slow smile, "since I've never had the privilege of beholding that sanctuary."

Her face tingled to pink as she said with an embarrassed laugh, "Of course not. Mom and Dad would have died if I'd invited a boy, even you, into my bedroom in high school!"

"They'd have died if they'd known what their daughter actually had in mind for 'even me' the night she graduated high school."

Callie pushed off from the rail. "*Why* do you keep bringing that up?" she cried. "Good grief, Drew, I was just a kid!"

He reached up to grasp the tips of her fingers. "Come on, Callie, I'm only teasing. Lord, it's easy to get a rise out of you."

"But why must you continually dredge up old history? I'm not the same person I was then." She looked down at him with pained eyes.

"No, you're not the same," he murmured. "You're definitely…something, though. Can you see now why I pushed you away? Even you just admitted you were only a kid."

She said nothing for a moment. It sounded, just slightly, as if he were trying to tell her something—as if he were apologizing. For what? She'd been the one at fault.

"I may have been a kid, but what I felt was real, no matter what." She tried, unsuccessfully, to free herself from his grasp. "I would have done anything for you, Drew Barnett."

"You think I don't know that, Callie? That I don't realize I'm the reason you left Iowa six years ago?" The breeze blew a shock of ebony hair across his forehead. "You wouldn't believe the number of times I've replayed that night in my mind, wondering how I could have responded differently and allowed you to feel you could stay."

He bent his head, as if bowing over the hand still clasped in his. Her position standing above him offered her the opportunity for a rare perspective, and Callie gave in to the desire to exhaust her study of him: the midnight black head above broad shoulders, the prominent cheekbones creating two ridges of flesh slightly paler than the rest of his face, the sweep of outlandishly long lashes on either side of a straight nose.

"And yet I wanted you to go," he went on, thumb rubbing the back of her fingers. "You *were* just a starry-eyed kid who deserved a chance to mature, see a little of the world, before making choices that would affect you the rest of your life. You deserved to dream a little longer, rather than have someone like me thrust reality on you. My reality."

He looked up at her. "I've always wondered, harsh as I was with you, if I didn't do that anyway—disillusion you. I never knew if your decision to go to California, made after that night, had done you good or more damage."

Drew smiled, shaking her fingers gently. "But when I saw you again, and talked to you, that was the first I knew for sure. Going away *had* been good for you. You've blossomed, grown up. And yet you still have that same spontaneous enthusiasm, even with all you're going through with your family. And I'm glad going to California worked out for you."

Again, she wanted to pull away, but the look in his azure eyes stopped her. He was glad, then, he'd rejected her, glad that she'd gone to California. When the time came, would he be glad to see her go back?

Would she?

She tried to dredge up the picture of him and Maura Foster that had haunted her imagination for days. Strangely, she couldn't locate that particular image at this moment.

Gently, Callie extracted her fingers from his grasp. "I'm glad, too, Drew," she said. *Glad—if there wasn't a reason then to stay. If there isn't one now.*

His gaze dove deeply into hers and she looked away, once again seeking to conceal her feelings from this man.

"Look, Callie, about breeding Pavlova—"

"The subject is closed, Drew," she said firmly. "I agree it's not feasible right now."

He stood. She refused to back up a step and found herself staring at his naked chest, for lack of a better place.

"Lord, you're stubborn," he sighed. "I'm not talking about payment, if that's the problem."

"It isn't," Callie replied stiffly. "It's too much work, and I won't be here to share the responsibility. I wouldn't dream of being so selfish."

"I know Nate won't mind. If you've got one horse to take care of, two's not much more expense or work."

"But it's still work. Perhaps the solution, then, is to sell Pavlova." Her lower lip trembled at the very idea.

"That's not what I was suggesting!" Drew gave a huff of exasperation. "Dammit, Callie, would it hurt to take a favor?"

She lifted her chin. "All right, I will, on one condition. You consider your obligation to help me out with the house fulfilled." One way or another, she'd get him out of her life. "I can't allow you to do so much."

She felt a twinge of contrition at the hurt in his eyes. "It's not much. Not at all. But suit yourself." His look of frustration was unmistakable as he frowned at her. "As of now, I owe you one roll in the hay by proxy—courtesy of Sancho."

Her mouth dropped open. "Really, Drew. Being a veterinarian does not give you leave to talk so offensively," she accused rashly, knowing that what she really wanted right now was any excuse to pick a fight. She wanted a reason, justification for driving him away, more than the fact that she didn't trust herself not to fall for him all over again.

"Offensive? Suggestive, maybe, but how was that offensive?" he protested.

"Well, did you imply...I mean you made it sound like—" she stammered, blushing in spite of herself. *Damn* him!

"Like what?" Drew asked. He lifted his arm and negligently propped his hand on the post behind her.

"Oh, you know what I mean," she said, cursing the breathless quality in her voice. "All your breeding talk and...all."

"It's my job, lady." His face was inches from hers. "And I've never known you to be shy about such matters before. Something change in the last six years?"

Callie swallowed. She couldn't answer him. How could he do this to her with just one look, one word? Any moment now, she'd give herself away, and he'd know how much he could move her.

"Something's changed, all right," Drew provided for her. He raised his hand and brushed a few damp straggles of hair away from her temple. "Such a fascinating bundle of contrasts you are: a little prudish, but still earthy. Shrewd, but trusting. Independent, but still...compliant." He paused. "Do you know what I think, Callie?"

She was riveted by that voice, by the glow in his indigo eyes. "Wh-what do you think?" she managed to ask, and realized the question hadn't sounded scornful, as she'd meant it to.

"I think," he said softly, "that you're right. It's time to put that long-ago evening—and the rest of the past—behind us, if we can, and start over." His face was somber. "Do you think that's possible?"

In the blink of an eye, she felt as if she'd turned a corner and a whole different view lay ahead of her. The denial of a moment ago vanished, for something had changed in the man who stood looking at her so earnestly. Much as he'd asked for her promise a few days ago to hold on to her dreams, he wanted something from her now. Another promise, though different. And he made her want to respond, though she wasn't quite sure what he asked of her.

"Anything's possible," Callie said.

She felt that somehow, she'd come up with an answer that pleased him, for he smiled then, fondly. "Hold that thought, Callie."

He shoved off from the post and briefly scrutinized the paint peeling on it, his hands propped loosely on his jeaned hips, the tail of his shirt billowing out behind him. Seeming to make up his mind about something, he cast an eye at her. "How about if I come by this evening with my horse trailer and we drive over to Nate's for Pavlova?"

Callie could only nod, still reacting to his closeness and feeling more confused than ever about Drew Barnett. So much for getting him out of her life.

"Fine. I'll be 'round about seven." He clattered down the steps and started across the yard to his truck.

She stepped forward, pressing her palms to either side of the wood pillar, and watched him go. Her heart lifted as his words sank in. Perhaps he'd meant nothing by it. But then . . .

Callie sighed. So it seemed they'd a pact to forget the past. Now all she had to worry about was the future.

Drew was right on time, and Callie trotted down the porch steps where she and Hannah had been awaiting his arrival. He reached across the cab to open the truck's door for her, smiling a greeting. Callie smiled back, then frowned as Hannah who, for all her bulk, hopped nimbly onto the wide bench seat.

"Hope you don't mind if she comes along," Callie said, sliding in next to the spaniel.

Drew laughed and rumpled the dog's black coat. "She's more than welcome."

Hannah barked her thanks and panted happily, shifting on the seat to get a steady purchase as the Bronco pitched over a pothole in the drive and out onto the gravel road.

Callie had to laugh also. "I think she's as anxious as I am to see Pavlova again." Her smile died on her lips as she cast Drew an embarrassed glance. "I mean, Hannah's just caught my excitement. Obviously, she doesn't understand what I'm feeling."

Drew grinned. "No need to be embarrassed because you told Hannah about bringing Pavlova home. Especially to *me*. Animals understand more than we think they do, Callie—and I think you know it."

She sent him a sheepish smile. "I *did* go on about it to her after you left." She didn't mention how his touch and his words had had her hugging Hannah with barely contained vigor. Now, she clasped her hands in her lap to suppress the unbidden elation that had suddenly sprung up in her.

"I shouldn't get my hopes up," she said before realizing the double meaning in her words. "I mean, I don't even know if Pavlova will remember me. After all, we had only a little while to get acquainted the last time I was home."

"It'll do. Seems like all it takes is a few minutes with you, and you can have any animal eating out of your hand." He smiled. "Literally."

"Yes, but for her to remember me—I don't know." She gave Hannah an absent scratch. "Seems like a lot to ask from a horse."

"Well, in this case, I'll put my money on you." He shook his head briefly. "You've got a way with animals, Callie. I think it's one of the things I've always loved about you."

Callie's hand froze in Hannah's fur. She continued to stare straight ahead, though inside, a secret desire made itself known, gave itself a name, told her it was the reason she'd been buoyed as if walking on air since this afternoon.

I've always loved that about you.

His words held no special significance, she told herself. It was just an expression. Still, the tone of his voice had been so quiet, so special. And after this afternoon... She wished she had the nerve to look at him, to try to discern the import of his words, but she was deathly afraid he'd read her own hopes in her eyes. *I've always loved...*

She wondered once again how to respond to him, if she should respond. Perhaps it was only her reacting so strongly, as she was apt to with him. Finally, she chose to gloss over the moment.

"I've been postponing going over to Nate's to see Pav," she said after a moment, "because I knew I'd want to spend half my time riding her instead of doing my work." She braved a glance his way. "Thanks for taking the time out to go get her."

"My pleasure," he said with a shrug. She'd been right. The fingers of one of his hands curled loosely around the steering wheel, and his arm was propped casually on the edge of the open window. Not a pose in which one made great revelations. "I've been meaning to take a look at her anyway."

"Oh? What for?" she asked, puzzled.

"Uh—" Drew cleared his throat. "You know, check out the goods for Sancho."

"Sure, whatever," Callie said. She didn't press him further, hesitant to renew the subject that'd seemed too intimate this afternoon.

To get to the window, Hannah abruptly planted two paws heavily on Callie's thigh. "Hannah!" Callie rubbed her leg and scooted across the seat to allow the dog access. Hannah thrust her head out the window, ears and tongue blowing backward in the wind.

"The little ingrate." Callie turned to Drew with a smile, only to find his face now just inches from hers. She dropped her chin and busied herself securing Hannah with her hand on the dog's collar as she felt her cheeks grow warm in the heat of his nearness.

"What's going on here?" Drew asked.

Callie, who'd taken refuge in watching the setting sun weave a loose fabric of violets and pinks on the horizon, turned back to him quizzically. "What?"

He smiled down at her, his black brows puckered in puzzlement. "You're glowing tonight. It's more than seeing Pavlova. Like you've got a secret."

She felt herself grow even rosier under his scrutiny. "Well, I did have a bit of good news today," she excused her blush. "My boss called. She's planning out the six-month forecast, and wanted to let me know I'd be in charge of the Redmond account. My first!" she said triumphantly.

"Congratulations, Callie." He gave her an approving nod. "If your excitement's any indication, this must be a big deal."

"Actually, it's a small account, but my very own."

Drew chuckled. "I meant it must be important to you."

"It is. My boss said she wanted me to know—" Callie stopped, remembering. Leslie, her boss, had told her the news, "Because," she'd said, "I don't want you falling in love with some gorgeous Hawkeye and abandoning me for life on the prairie without at least thinking about it twice."

Callie shrugged uncomfortably at the memory. "It's an incentive." She averted her gaze once more, lest Drew detect her thoughts. "And a small success for this little fish in a big pond."

"I see." From the corner of her eye, she saw him study her, then shift his gaze back to the road. "It must be very different there. In Los Angeles, I mean."

"One of Los Angeles's biggest industries is being different," Callie agreed, glad for the neutral topic. "I've gotten used to it now, but I'll never forget what it was like, seeing Venice Beach for the first time." She gave a short laugh. "You know, the first time I went to Disneyland, it was truly like entering a Magic Kingdom. All those years of seeing the place on television—I realized once I was there that, when a child, I'd never dreamed of actually going to Disneyland. From my little farmhouse in Iowa, I couldn't conceive of it as actually existing."

She slid Drew a droll look. "I suppose that sounds incredibly naive."

"Not at all. It does give me a clue as to why you've stayed in California all these years."

"It does?"

"Well, who wouldn't enjoy living in the place of their dreams?"

"I wouldn't exactly call it that," Callie pointed out. "I think everyone knows California's no paradise."

"True. But it offers you something I think you wouldn't have found in Iowa if you'd stayed—a real challenge. In California, there'll always be another level of achievement to try for, to motivate you and keep you interested."

"Well, it's certainly true it'll take me a few years to rise to the top of that cream pitcher," she said amicably. "But I'm finding it very rewarding to take on the relatively simple task of renovating Mom and Dad's house. Promotions and account control are all very stimulating, but this inn is...personal. What I do at the inn, I feel right here." She laid her hand over her heart and looked up at Drew, so close beside her. "And that's the challenge and the reward, you know?"

"I certainly do, Callie." His eyes were deep-water blue as he regarded her. And like deep water, she felt herself sink into them. He turned back to his driving and she caught her breath, as if indeed she'd been immersed. He could do that to her, so quickly.

She searched for something to say. "You know, I didn't let Nate know we were coming."

"No problem. I gave him a call." Drew cocked two fingers in greeting at a passing vehicle. "He picked up a cherry pie at the café this afternoon and said he supposed he'd have to share a piece with us. He was kind of put out." He chuckled. "I can sympathize. Those pies of Maura's are something else."

Callie felt a jolt of surprise at the name. "Maura Foster?"

Drew nodded as the Bronco vibrated over a section of washboardlike road. "You remember Maura? She was a few grades behind Nate and me. She's been selling pies to the café to make some extra money." He frowned slightly. "God knows she can use the cash."

Callie managed to control her features. How could she have forgotten about Drew and Maura?

"Ever since Wayne was killed in that accident at the co-op, Maura's been struggling to make ends meet," Drew went on, seemingly oblivious to her silence. "Her boy's only four, you know. Cute kid. Maura'd get a job in one of the larger towns around, but Davey's taking his dad's death pretty hard, and she hates to leave him for long stretches." Drew glanced at Callie, a worried line between his brows, and she raised her own eyebrows.

"I'm sure it must be difficult for her," she murmured as disappointment and an ensuing annoyance at that disappointment swept over her. She could barely believe she'd allowed herself to get all excited about a few innocent comments by Drew, when the reality of it was he cared for Maura.

He concentrated on his driving again, chewing the side of his mouth thoughtfully. "Callie—" Another glance at her, quick and searching. "Have you thought about running your inn yourself?"

"Me?" she blurted out, surprised more by his abrupt change of subject than the subject itself.

"Why not you?" He slowed to turn into Nate's driveway, and Hannah bumped against her, forcing Callie against Drew. "You just admitted that you find working on it personally rewarding. Wouldn't you like to stay and run it, too, instead of hiring a proprietor?"

"But Mom and Dad are coming back in the fall," Callie protested. "They need all the income from the inn they can get. And someday Nate will marry and have a family to support. They don't need to support me, as well."

"Oh. Well, maybe you could help others start their own bed-and-breakfast places. I'd think the more the better, otherwise some big motel chain is going to come in, if they think there's a market. And that wouldn't help your parents' prospects."

"I suppose I could do something like that for a while, but even that occupation has a limited longevity," she answered a little more curtly than she meant to. But what was he getting at? Why all the questions about the inn? Of course, on the surface it would seem reasonable for Callie to take over the inn until her parents came back. They'd argued in much the same way this winter when she'd verified that she could take a leave of absence. But then, she'd known what her parents' motives were. They wanted their daughter back in Iowa for good, and the inn provided a nice solution. While Drew...

He'd stopped the truck next to Nate's house and turned toward her, looping his arm across the top of the steering wheel, the other stretched along the back of the seat. She studied him. The expression in his eyes seemed almost hopeful.

"What if you started a reservation service or something between the different inns?" he persisted. "You could charge a small commission on each reservation."

"With a number of inns, a referral network would certainly be practical," she said, for the moment going along with his reasoning. He'd obviously put some thought into the matter, and she began to wonder if, after all, there was more behind his remarks than curiosity. "But whoever ran it wouldn't have time to run an inn too. Not single-handedly. And until Mom and Dad came back, we'd still need a proprietor."

Drew paused, whether in thought or hesitation, she couldn't tell. "Well, what about Maura?" he asked.

Callie stared at him. Yes, what about Maura?

Drew's face faded as the image of him and Maura that had eluded her earlier now sprang in living color to her mind. Maura, a pure-faced woman with fair hair and skin, and angelic eyes. So unlike Callie. She couldn't prevent herself from remembering Maura's sweet smile, perhaps now changed forever. How she must have suffered to lose a husband so young! And now, to be struggling so, needful of a helping hand...

With a blast of comprehension, Callie realized the purpose behind Drew's questioning. Her inn needed a proprietor. Maura Foster filled the bill to a *T.* If Callie were definitely out of the picture, with no intention of returning, then who better, in Drew's mind, to take her place?

"With Maura, it could work then, couldn't it, Callie?"

With effort, she focused on the man before her. He hadn't moved a muscle, his gaze penetrating, the concern in it so real, as if everything depended on her answer.

Everything for Maura. Not Callie.

Somehow, she kept herself still, resisting the urge to shrink away—though not from Drew, but from herself, for once again being so foolish. And, she realized with sinking spirit, for letting herself nourish her old infatuation for him. For despite her rationalizations, her resistance and her reluctance, somehow her fixation on Drew Barnett had grown as intense again as it had been at seventeen. It must be, otherwise she wouldn't now feel the tug of tiny roots being pulled loose and shaken in shock.

She nodded her head slowly. "Yes, Drew. A network of inns—it could work, and I'd be glad to help people get organized, but of course that's all I could do. I'm only here for two months, after all." She gazed at him levelly. "Then I go back to California for good."

His brows drew together over eyes that grew even more blue at her words. Then he nodded, looking away. "I understand," he said. "You've got a great job there, a lot to look forward to. Why would you ever come back to stay?"

Why indeed? she wondered.

Chapter Six

Nate stood bent over a greasy piece of machinery as Callie and Drew entered the barn. Tools were strewn around him, and Nate cursed softly and steadily as he picked up and discarded one after another. He looked up at their muffled steps in the straw.

"Hey, Callie, Drew," he greeted them, straightening. Pulling a rag from his hip pocket, he wiped his hands.

"Hello, Nate." Callie gave her brother a quick hug.

Nate shook Drew's hand. A questioning glance passed between the two men.

Drew nodded toward the machinery Nate had been working on. "Can I give you a hand?"

"Naw." Nate stuffed the rag back into his pocket. "Durned thing's pretty hopeless. I just thought I'd give it another shot before I replaced it." He gave his sister an understanding smile. "Besides, I bet you didn't come here to help me wrestle with this crankcase. Someone's been waiting for you, Callie."

The three of them started toward the back of the barn.

"Oh, I doubt if Pavlova will know who I am, after so long," Callie protested once again, even as her feet carried her swiftly toward the stall. After her conversation with Drew, something about putting her arms around a creature who would love her without condition seemed infinitely comforting.

"I told you, Callie," Nate said. "You always get all the animals to love you, even that old sow I raised for 4-H one year. Durnedest thing, remember that, Drew?"

Callie didn't hear Drew's reply as she ran the rest of the way to the stall. It was dim in that corner of the barn, but she could see the mare's eyes gleam in the indistinct light and the horse's ears pricked forward at the sound of Callie's soft step.

"Pav," she called faintly as she approached. "Hey, Pav, remember me? Remember Callie?" When she reached the stall, she simply stood before it, talking softly and steadily, in case the mare failed to recognize her voice and scent.

But Pavlova nickered and moved restlessly forward, her large head searching eagerly for Callie's touch. Callie laid her small hand along the mare's smooth nose and curled her arm up and around Pavlova's velvet brown neck. "That's right, Pav. It's me. It's Callie. I'm . . . I'm home," she whispered quietly into the mare's ear.

Nate and Drew by that time had reached the stall and were watching them both.

Callie glanced at them. "I don't believe it," she said. "She does remember me—or maybe it's just my wishful thinking."

"Nope," Nate assured her, "you're her girl all right. She knows you. Amazing, isn't it?"

She laughed at Nate's words. When Pavlova's nose nudged downward on her right side, she *was* amazed. "What makes you think there might be something in that old pocket, girl?" she crooned and pulled a small apple from it. "You're too smart for your own good, aren't you?" She balanced the round fruit on her open palm while Pavlova daintily crunched into it.

She turned from the horse excitedly. "Nate, you've got my tack here, don't you? Would you help me saddle her? I can't wait to get on her." ·

The two men exchanged glances.

"Well, now, Callie, that's probably not a good idea right now," Drew began.

"Not a good idea?" Callie swung open the stall and stepped inside. "What do you mean?" Glancing around the gloomy interior, she located a currying brush hung on the corner post, and she caught it up and began grooming the horse.

"Pavlova's not up to a lot of exercise right now," Nate helped Drew out.

"She isn't?" Callie paused in her routine to stare in alarm at her brother, then Drew. "She's not sick, is she, Drew? Is that why you wanted to look at her? Why didn't you tell me?"

Drew leaned his forearms on the edge of the stall. "Calm down. Pavlova's fine. If she weren't, I'd have told you."

Callie eyed him warily over her shoulder. She found a clean saddle blanket and hoisted it onto the smooth chestnut expanse. "Guess what, Nate. Drew's going to breed Pav to his stallion."

"Do tell!" was Nate's amazed response.

"By next year, the inn will not only have a beautiful mare, but also a beautiful little . . ."

Her voice trailed off and Callie paused in her ministrations, her hand running along Pavlova's smooth side. "Gosh, she's gotten fat!" she exclaimed. "Nate, have you been overfeeding her like you did Hannah? Honestly, I thought you knew better than that. Nothing is more unfair to an animal, right, Drew?"

"Right," Drew agreed. "Nate does know better. Don't you, Nate?"

"All right, I've had just about my fill of your bull roar, Barnett," Nate said, hooking a booted foot on a wood slat and giving his friend a knowing, tolerant look. "I did my part by keeping it a secret, but I'll be durned if I'll stand by while you pussyfoot around telling her at my expense."

Callie turned. The two of them stood side by side with the same expression of mild chicanery on their faces that had dominated their thirty-year friendship. "Tell me what?" she demanded, her suspicion instantly aroused.

"Well, Callie," Drew began, "Pavlova's not fat, exactly."

"No?" She glanced at him, and then at her brother. "You don't call this fat?"

"Oh, durn it, Drew," Nate burst out, obviously enjoying Drew's discomfiture a little bit. He turned to Callie. "Sancho's already visited the lady here."

"What?" she sputtered, though she managed to grasp her brother's meaning just as he confirmed it.

"Pavlova's pregnant, kiddo."

Callie's fingers closed on the edge of the heavy blanket and it slid off Pavlova's back into a pile at her feet as her arms went heavily limp. Her eyes flew to Drew's sheepish face while her own flamed. So Nate had known about Pavlova from the beginning and had thought it would be great fun to see her earnestly seek Drew out about breeding her. And Drew had obligingly led her on, just for kicks! He *knew* Pavlova was already with foal when he'd made his "deal" with her. Obviously it would have been much too humdrum to have simply told her Pavlova had been bred—not when they had the opportunity to hit such an easy mark as her.

To her horror, Callie felt tears of frustration sting her eyes. She stooped to retrieve the blanket and replaced it on Pavlova's back, not facing them and fighting for composure.

Even knowing she was taking the situation too much to heart, she still felt unaccountably wounded. *It's just a harmless joke,* she told herself over and over, but after the events of today with Drew, it seemed to drive home his true view of her. To him, she was and always would be Nate's little sister, teasable, headstrong. An impulsive child who jumped to conclusions and had to be shown that what she wanted all along was right in the palm of her hand. Once and for all, she realized no amount of time in any sophisticated city would change the image of her Drew held in his mind. They could agree to put the past behind them, but there was too much history between them. It would have been like trying not to be Nate's sister—she just was and always would be. She would never catch up to either of them, as she'd so greatly desired since she was old enough to think.

And she would never change so much that she might be a Maura Foster.

She turned, determined to be a good sport though she could barely summon a smile. "You two old bachelors!" she chided with a laugh. "Nothing better to do with yourselves! If you put half the effort and thought you put into your little jokes into something worthwhile, we'd probably have a cure for cancer by now. I'm hardly one to judge though." She cocked her index finger at her temple. "I actually thought Pav was *fat!*"

Her voice cracked on that last word, along with her facade, and she saw expressions of surprise, then contrition cross the two men's faces before, once more, she took refuge in her ministrations to Pavlova. She began smoothing the already creaseless blanket. "Shh," she soothed the horse, who, despite Callie's bright tone, had picked up on the distress in her mistress's voice and nickered restlessly.

The poor animal, Callie thought. The pattern on the blanket blurred before her eyes. She blinked fiercely. "Shh. It's okay, girl."

"Callie—" Drew said from behind her.

"You know what'd be nice?" she interrupted, feeling drained after the profusion of emotions that had rocketed through her in the past few hours. "A few minutes alone with my horse."

She stroked and cooed to Pavlova and heard but one set of receding footsteps. She wondered who had stayed. She didn't have to wonder for long.

"I do have an explanation, Callie," Drew murmured.

Callie's chin rose and she took a deep breath. "What's to explain? No explanation necessary, really, Drew."

Drew entered the stall and stepped to the other side of Pavlova. Though now facing him, Callie obstinately kept her gaze fastened on her task.

"When your parents heard about my buying Sancho last year," he said as if she hadn't spoken, "they gave me a call about breeding Pavlova. They thought it would be a nice surprise for you this spring when you came to visit." He ran expert hands over the mare as he talked. "I think they intended to tell you eventually, so you could time your visit to coincide with the foaling, but with your father's illness . . . Well, when it all came about that you'd be back here this spring anyway, they decided to make it a real surprise for you."

Out of the corner of her eye, she saw him glance at her. She still refused to look at him, but found her eyes following the movement of his large hands, gentle but firm on the mare's flesh. "They asked Nate and me to keep it a secret until you got here. Nate would've told you about her pregnancy before now, but you were so excited about seeing Pavlova, it wouldn't have been the same, telling you. We were going to get you over here eventually, especially after you started talking about breeding her, but you wanted to wait. And you kept going on about breeding her."

"I see," Callie said slowly. She felt like the five-year-old on Christmas morning whom everyone has conspired to keep believing in Santa just one more year. "So my parents already paid you for Sancho's services, and all that baloney about making a deal with me was just egging me on for the sake of a 'surprise.'"

"Yes and no," Drew said, his melodious voice low and soothing, perhaps as much to appease her as to calm the mare, whose ears still twitched nervously at the undertone in their words. "I received not a penny of payment from your parents, and I didn't expect any. I wouldn't have expected any from you, either."

"But why that whole charade today, Drew?" she asked, finally looking at him, unable to disguise her hurt any longer. "It had nothing to do with surprising me."

"I know." Drew's voice was thoughtful. He stood in front of Pavlova now, running his palm from forelock to nostrils in a repetitive motion. He caught Callie's eyes on him and smiled slightly, as if puzzled.

"I guess I was irritated because you seemed not to want my help, first when I stopped by the day you were hoeing weeds out front, and then this afternoon. When you lit into me about teasing you, then made such a point of wishing me gone for good, I guess I got a little testy myself."

He gave Pavlova a final pat. "I didn't do it to play a joke on you. You just...got to me. Once I saw what I'd done this afternoon, shooting off my mouth, I wanted to bring you over here as soon as possible to rectify the situation."

He leaned against the inside of the stall, three fingers of each hand crammed into his jeans pockets, and gave her a sideways glance. "Why don't you want my help, Callie?"

She flushed, grinding her fists into her own pockets. "It's not that I don't want *your* help," she lied softly. "I just ... this project is very important to me. I can't help but be a little possessive about it. It's my chance to do something for my family that no one else can do. I thought you knew that."

"And this is my chance to give your family back a bit of the support you gave mine. I thought you knew that." He hunched his shoulders in thought. "Callie, I know how hard it is to put aside the dreams and ambitions in your life to take care of your family. I've been there, but if I succeeded, I didn't do it alone. I owe that to your family. So now, does it seem so odd I might want to help you and Nate if I can? Good grief, Callie, you two are more than just friends, you're—"

"Like brother and sister to you?" Callie finished for him. Somehow the words were easier to bear coming from her instead of him.

He seemed about to disagree, but something in her expression stopped him. "All right, like family. And I don't think I could live with myself if I didn't give you both whatever assistance I could." He looked away for a moment, concentrating his gaze into the gloom in the back of the barn. Then he turned to her again. "I'm sorry I messed up the surprise for you. I'm sorry it seemed I was baiting you in some way. I . . . I'm sorry, Callie."

By now, most of her hurt had passed as Callie stood listening to Drew's explanations. She understood, of course, that he hadn't meant her any harm. She understood, also, that he was motivated only by a wish to help her and Nate—the sister and brother he had never had—as they had helped him. And she'd been ungraciously, ungratefully pushing him away from the moment she'd stepped onto Iowa soil again because she nursed some perverse fascination for him that wasn't his fault.

The situation was just as she'd perceived in the beginning. Drew, neighbor and friend, was nothing more than that. Whatever she'd read into his words or gestures had been her own wild imaginings.

She looked up at him. "When's Pavlova due?" she asked, the closest she'd allow to absolution.

"June. Maybe late May."

Her heart lifted despite herself, dissolving some of the pain. "Then maybe I *will* be here when she foals," she murmured, revealing her hope to Drew. "I would have hated to miss it."

She looked at him as he lounged against the stall, his heel hooked on a rail. He smiled in reconciliation, and she grudgingly smiled back.

"And you wonder why I'm not dying to move back here and expose myself to this sort of treatment on a regular basis," she wisecracked, trying for a lighter tone.

"Surf bums and Disneyland can hold one's interest for only so long," he remarked. He cocked his head toward the door. "We'd better get in there before Nate wolfs down that entire pie."

Callie chose to remain silent rather than reveal that eating Maura Foster's cherry pie appealed not in the least to her at that moment. But she'd decided to be game about Maura and whatever her relationship with Drew. She'd get over any lingering feelings of disappointment she had in tonight's outcome. And she'd get over Drew and the silly infatuation she'd begun to build up again.

They trooped into the house and found Nate sitting at his kitchen table, a mug of coffee grasped between his palms. The pie sat uncut upon it, with three plates and forks beside the admittedly delicious-looking pastry.

Her brother gave her a chagrined smile. "Everything okay, kiddo?"

She saw instantly that he regretted the misunderstanding between them. For all the visible absorption that made him seem oblivious to others and their concerns, Nate was a sensitive man who'd never hurt another—human or animal—on purpose.

"Drew explained," she said with an answering smile. "Sorry I'm so touchy—but you know me. And your surprise really is one of the best I've ever had. It's what I've wanted ever since Mom and Dad bought Pavlova for me."

Nate stood and grinned with relief. He shrugged. "Well, seems you always get whatever you want, doesn't it? Durned if I know how you do it, from a couple thousand miles away."

If you only knew, she thought. But Callie made a dismissing sound with her mouth before she gave her brother a big hug. "Thanks, Nate," she said into his ear.

"You're welcome. Although it was Mom and Dad's idea. All I did was take care of her till you got here." He released her and nodded at Drew. "Drew here's the one who did all the real work." Nate coughed discreetly. "Him and Sancho, that is."

Drew stood with one hip propped against Nate's antiquated refrigerator, topping it by a foot and a half. He smiled gently at Callie.

"Thanks, too, Drew," she said hesitantly. And then, because he stood but a few feet away, because she'd given Nate a hug and now to omit such a physical gesture—especially with a friend who'd done so much—would seem awkward, Callie found herself in Drew's embrace.

It was so innocent. And yet, as her arms tightened briefly about his waist, as his own arms spanned her back in an answering squeeze, as his cheek pressed with controlled urgency against her temple, Callie knew once and for all she was a bigger fool than she'd ever dreamed of being. For as she buried her face against his shoulder, she realized her feelings for Drew Barnett had really gone beyond infatuation, beyond a crush.

Thank God, she thought, pulling away from him the instant it seemed appropriate. Thank God she hadn't been so foolish as to make some silly declaration as she had over six years ago.

She stood apart from Drew awkwardly, wanting to retreat without seeming too obviously disturbed by his nearness. *He doesn't even know the predicament you've gotten yourself into.* Again, she thanked heaven, for the gift of Drew's ignorance.

"Well, how about a piece of Maura's pie?" Nate asked from behind her. Callie turned, but not before her shifting gaze collided briefly with Drew's. She remembered how she'd bragged to him about the quality of her own pies. As if one's baking acumen directly correlated to one's ability to be loved by Drew Barnett.

She didn't allow herself to dwell on that thought, but set herself to dishing out pie and making animated conversation for the rest of the evening, though she choked down but a few bites of cherry pie.

It really *was* a waste, Callie made herself concede later within the sanctuary of her small room, when sleep eluded her. Maura's pie was definitely melt-in-your-mouth delicious. Nate had had two pieces, as well as the rest of hers.

And Drew's.

Chapter Seven

"How about a rutabaga festival?"

Otie Slater, Soldier Creek's mayor, glanced nervously around at the ten or so people assembled in Cora Lawsen's painfully tidy living room. "We could call it Rutabaga Days."

Cora pursed her lips at such a suggestion, obviously regarding it as highly ridiculous. "That'd be just dandy, Otie, but I don't know one person around here—and none of the farmers—with a rutabaga crop."

"What about pumpkins?" Ned Jones, owner of the dry-goods store, piped up. "Shorty Grimes grew that two-hundred-fifty-pound one, two years back. Got his picture in the *Sycamore County Times*."

"Sewardton's doing pumpkins," Cora dismissed Ned's offering succinctly.

"Squash?" someone put in.

"Done. By Selma," said Cora.

"How about Cornhusker Days?" Elbert Janes offered. He received a censuring look all around for that one. Although corn was a major crop, Iowa held a lively and not always good-spirited rivalry with neighboring Nebraska, whose college football team was nicknamed the Cornhuskers. A Cornhusker anything in Iowa would go over like a lead balloon.

"Well, then, how about soybeans?" Elbert asked defiantly, soybeans being another of Iowa's biggest crops and currently without a patron state. "You can't tell me some town's already come up with a Soybean Fest?"

Cora looked dubious. "I'll have to check. I know Morrisburg was thinking about it."

"At this rate," Drew leaned over to Callie and whispered, "every garden-variety vegetable will have its day."

Callie hid a smile behind the cover of a cough. This was the first meeting of the yet-to-be-named committee in charge of organizing the yet-to-be-named event to lure tourists to Soldier Creek. Each of the committee members had been asked, wheedled, or otherwise coerced into participating by Cora Lawsen, though most had business interests that would benefit from such an endeavor. The new lake and recreation area was the biggest thing to hit the county in twenty years and the perfect opportunity for its inhabitants to capitalize on an increase in visitors. Unfortunately, few residents were adept at promoting tourism or even in civic organizing. Except, perhaps, Cora Lawsen.

Callie had arrived late and out of breath to the meeting five minutes before. Her return to regular respiration had been further hampered by seeing Drew's smiling face as he scooted his chair closer to Hank Peterson's, on his right, and made room for Callie on his left. It had been only a few days since the episode with Pavlova, and upon seeing Drew, her heart seemed intent on pounding against the inside of her chest walls, as if desperate to get out. Callie realized it would take time for her feelings for Drew to settle, and only by seeing him, working with him and treating him like the neighbor and friend he was, would she come to terms with those emotions.

It'll pass, she told herself. *You got over him once, you can do it again.* He made it darned difficult, though, when he smiled at her with those blue eyes.

Cora Lawsen, her meringue white hair in tight, perfect pin curls surrounding a still peaches-and-cream face, surveyed each individual like a teacher who'd just asked a particularly complicated geometry question. "Come on, people. We need to come up with a theme for our event. Soldier Creek cannot allow Soldier Lake to open without some sort of recognition."

"How about something to do with heritage?" Drew suggested. "Bloomfield's going to have a Norwegian celebration. And Armstrong is planning its centennial."

"Ten years early, I've heard," Cora said. "But that's an excellent suggestion, Andrew." She turned her penetrating gaze on Callie. "What's your impression?" she asked, as if calling on Callie to recite next.

Callie shifted in her chair. Cora had told her over the phone that she expected Callie, being from California, to be a font of ideas—as if they grew on trees there but could not thrive in the climes of Iowa. Callie had gamely put her mind to the task.

"I think Drew's right," she said, with an acknowledging smile at him. "Most of the visitors to the lake are going to be fellow Iowans. By centering a celebration on history and heritage—say Pioneer Days—you create a sense of coming home, within your own state. People are always interested in discovering something about themselves. They like to know they came from somewhere, that they're carrying on tradition and that maybe someone will remember them when they're gone. And they want to know what makes them different, what makes them Iowans."

She looked inward as she spoke, trying to verbalize her feelings, calling upon those she felt so strongly herself. "That's what we're trying for with the Farrell Family Inn. If Soldier Creek itself could create that atmosphere—of going back to the simple pleasures, with those pleasures being the best and most heartfelt," she glanced around the group and grinned suddenly, "we'll draw people like flies."

Murmurs of approval drifted around the room.

"We could have old-time farming demonstrations or something," Otie Slater said.

"In period costume," added Myra Bledsoe, owner of Myra's Maid Rite Café. "I'd be willing to sponsor a butter-churning contest."

"My Frank's grandpa's 1939 John Deere tractor has sat out in the barn under a tarp for years," said Lettie Johnson. "Frank would die for an excuse to fix it up."

"We could have an antique quilt show at the town hall!"

The suggestions flew as momentum built for Callie's idea.

"Tell them about the bed-and-breakfast referral service," Drew said to her, under cover of conversation.

"But I wouldn't be able to oversee it," Callie protested in a whisper.

"You could at least bring it up, if only for people to kick around."

"Nossir. You know Cora. If I bring it up, I'll end up—" Her objections were arrested when she noticed Cora's perceptive eye on the two of them.

"You have another suggestion, Callie?" Cora asked, and the discussion died immediately. Everyone fixed their gaze on Callie as if she held prophesy over them.

"Actually, Drew and I have one." She fastened him with a *you're in this with me* look. "You all know why my family is starting an inn. We don't hope to make a fortune, just enough to supplement farming." Nods of sympathy encouraged her. "But Drew brought up an interesting consideration the other day. Most people who come to the lake will camp there, maybe because no alternatives are offered to them. My family's inn will offer one, but it'd be so much better for return business if we didn't have to turn people away when the inn is booked."

She sat forward in her chair. "What Drew suggested is that others in Soldier Creek get into the inn business. Now," she held up a hand as skeptical contention went up, "that doesn't mean people have to completely renovate their houses. Most of you live in well-maintained prairie-style homes with lots of character. Most of you have a spare bedroom or den or sewing room. I'd be willing to share my experiences in getting my family's inn going. With a little work, you could rent out one or two rooms every now and then, without disrupting your lives. And make a little money with very little cash outlay.''

Drew spoke up then, proposing the rest of the idea. ''If we set up a referral network, then all the calls for reservations would come through one phone number. Reservations would be made for the different inns, maybe on a rotating basis to give everyone a fair shake. People make one call, and they get a reservation.''

''What about when my mother-in-law comes for her yearly month-long visit?'' Elbert asked. ''There goes not only the spare bedroom but the whole house and neighborhood!''

Drew laughed along with everyone else. ''Then just let the network know your room isn't available for that time period.''

He neatly fielded additional objections, occasionally deferring to Callie's expertise, and soon the room fell silent as each person mentally rearranged furniture. Drew gave Callie a wink and she smiled, impressed with his strategy and grateful in spite of her initial misgivings. He was right, of course. The more alternative lodging in one area they could provide, the better her inn's chances. Faced with the news of no availability, people would find lodging somewhere else. A host of inns in town would keep visitors coming back to Soldier Creek again and again.

''Well,'' Cora said after a moment, ''shall we vote on holding a Soldier Creek Pioneer Days over a three-day period this summer?'' she asked, as if this were actually a democratic process. The motion was made, though, and duly voted. Cora triumphantly printed, in perfect penmanship, Pioneer Days Planning Committee on the white board behind her, as if setting it in stone. In Callie's opinion, Cora missed her calling when she had not become a teacher. Or perhaps a five-star general.

Cora turned back to the group and immediately disposed of the first matter of business by naming Callie head of the Bed and Breakfast subcommittee.

This was exactly what she'd been afraid would happen, Callie thought, her heart sinking. She might be able to educate people on starting their own B&B before she left, but alone she would never be able to attend to all the business aspects of starting a referral service in that time frame. "Oh, but I can't—" she began, only to be interrupted by Drew.

"I volunteer to serve on Callie's subcommittee," he raised his hand. "Hank will too."

He nudged Hank Peterson, who'd been dozing conspicuously throughout the meeting. The older man shook his gray head at his name, rousing himself. "Whatever you say, Cora," he mumbled.

Everyone laughed but Callie. Drew caught her pensive expression and laid a hand on her arm.

"I'll ask Maura to participate, too," he said reassuringly. "We'll get things organized in no time, working together."

Callie nodded, though her spirits plummeted further at his assurances. Yes, Maura Foster would be a welcome addition. Callie could imagine Drew, Hank, Maura and herself, all together, working against the time when Callie would leave and it would be the three of them to carry on without her.

This was exactly what she'd been afraid of.

With Cora at the helm, the rest of the committee's business went just as swiftly, and the meeting broke up at a little after ten o'clock. Callie had stopped to chat a moment with Myra Bledsoe and was just getting into her pickup when the screech of tires brought heads around. A car careened around the corner and barreled down the road toward them, creating such discordant noise in the peaceful town that half a dozen porch lights flicked on up and down the street.

The vehicle squealed to a stop and Callie saw Wally Carlson shoot from it, his eyes frantic and searching in the faint illumination of a nearby street lamp.

"Doc Barnett!" he said. "Is Doc Barnett here?"

Drew's large silhouette detached itself from the shadows. "What's the problem, Wally?"

"It's my son's pup, Doc." He gestured to the dark interior of the car, where Callie could see a small, pale face with big eyes staring back. "Rusty got out of his run and wandered onto the main road." Wally swallowed. "Car only glanced him, but it must have hit him pretty hard."

Everyone glanced at each other in the obscure light. It didn't sound good.

Nevertheless, Drew stepped forward and peered into Wally's car. "You've got the animal with you?"

"Yes. Jimmy's holding him still as he can. The dog doesn't seem to be bleeding anywhere, but...I don't know if you can do anything for the pup, Doc, but I'd appreciate your trying."

Drew nodded even as he headed for his Bronco. "Meet me at the clinic."

Callie watched the two vehicles drive off, taillights streaking red. She swallowed against the lump in her throat. Poor dog. Poor little boy. She felt their anguish as if it were her own, and wished there was something she could do. Thank God, at least, for Drew's clinic, which a mere twelve months ago had not existed. The pup would have the best care possible. Drew would have a time of it, though, trying to treat the animal's injuries without assistance.

Perhaps, she thought, she could help. Callie got into her truck and followed the cars up Second Avenue toward Main Street and Drew's clinic.

The situation was just as she'd guessed. Wally stood anxiously in the waiting room, clutching his son to him and murmuring reassurances to the boy. Callie swept past them into the corridor, spotting a door that said Surgery.

She opened it without knocking and found Drew bending over a stainless-steel table, the unmoving Rusty on its surface.

"Drew, I've come to—" She was interrupted by the look on Drew's face as he turned it toward her.

"Don't look, Callie," he snapped, still hunched over his patient. "Get out of here. Now!"

Callie took an involuntary step backward, shocked by Drew's countenance. His face was dark red with effort, his black brows nearly joined above his eyes, reflecting his intense preoccupation. She felt exactly as Beauty must have, coming upon Beast in the throes of his savage obsession. But why would Drew want to keep her from seeing him? Or was it that he wanted to keep her from seeing the injured dog? After her actions of a few weeks ago when she'd brought Hannah in for treatment, she could see how he might want to shield her. He knew how greatly she loved animals and that she couldn't stand to see one suffer.

And yet Drew loved animals, too. It was why he'd become a veterinarian. And he needed her help, such as it was, if he were to have a chance of saving this one.

Callie closed the door behind her and advanced to the examining table. "I thought you might need a hand," she said.

"Then comfort Jimmy," he said, his hands working furiously. He'd already put an oxygen mask on the half-grown retriever and was quickly establishing an IV line in the animal's left front leg.

"Jimmy's got Wally," Callie said succinctly. "You need me."

He glanced up at her. Callie stared calmly back. He apparently decided he hadn't time to argue with her, for he jerked his head toward a cupboard on one wall. "Top left shelf. Lactated Ringers. It's labeled."

Callie moved quickly to the cupboard and snatched up a plastic pouch, returning to his side. Drew hung the pouch on a nearby IV stand, attaching it to the catheter in Rusty's leg. The retriever lay still, panting in short but heavy breaths, his eyes open and staring blankly. He didn't even react when Drew administered a shot of what Callie thought was some kind of painkiller.

"Steroids," Drew corrected her, upon her question. "He's in shock. We've got to get him stabilized."

Callie nodded, glad Drew had said "we." She refrained from further questions, ready to provide assistance as she hovered close to the disturbingly inert animal while Drew, starting at the dog's head, began examining its body. With hands gentle but probing, he felt for fractures or other injuries. As Wally had said, the dog had no open wounds, and no limbs seemed to be broken, but Callie noticed the retriever seemed deathly pale around the gums and inside its red-gold ears. When Drew opened Rusty's mouth, Callie was stunned to see that the dog's tongue had gone completely white.

Its abdomen seemed tight as drum, and when Drew palpated it, Rusty yipped sharply and struggled to rise.

"Hold him still," Drew said. Callie, glad for something to do, held the dog gently but firmly as Drew continued his examination. He worked against time, yet he was thorough, and she realized no more than five minutes had passed since she'd come through the door.

Finished with his nose-to-tail examination, Drew rechecked the animal's vital signs. "He's not stabilizing," he muttered, almost to himself. Abruptly, he grabbed a syringe and with a quick swab of alcohol, stabbed the needle into Rusty's abdomen.

Callie's head spun sickly as the syringe filled with blood, but she held on to the dog, blinking rapidly to regain her equilibrium. She met Drew's gaze over the animal's body. "What is it?" she asked.

"Spleen or liver," he answered, and from his tone Callie knew that something was terribly wrong. "One or both's been ruptured."

"Can you do something? Stop the bleeding or hemorrhaging or whatever?" She was grasping at straws and she knew it. She knew nothing of veterinary medicine. Her father and brother had done most of the nonemergency doctoring on the livestock, the birthing and vaccinating. Even if she'd been skilled in that kind of care, injuries were an entirely different problem.

"I can try." He strode to the cupboard, grabbing another of the clear plastic pouches and what looked like an Ace bandage. Returning to the table, he opened another IV catheter in the dog's other front leg before beginning to wrap the bandage around Rusty's abdomen. Sweat poured down Drew's face and neck as he directed Callie to turn the dog or hold it still. Within moments, he'd wrapped the abdomen in a constricting binding. He lifted the dog's lip and peered at its gums.

"Come on, boy," he said. "Help me out here. Just a little color, just a small sign you're stabilizing, and I can get in there."

Rusty raised his head weakly at Drew's words, brown eyes willing to the last. His tail lifted in a feeble wag. Then he laid his head back down, his eyes closing. And with a soft groan, like air being pushed from a bellows, the dog stopped breathing.

Callie's own breath caught painfully in her throat. "Oh, Drew," she whispered disbelievingly. She'd never felt more useless or helpless as she watched Drew slowly straighten and lay a soothing hand on Rusty's head. Drew's gaze traveled around the brightly lit room. He looked tired, infinitely tired, those blue eyes of his a dull slate color.

"All this equipment," he said softly. "And not a damned thing I could do."

He removed the IVs and all other signs of the struggle for life that had just taken place in the room. Unfolding a surgical drape, he pulled it up over the dog so that only Rusty's head and shoulders showed. Then he stepped out of the surgery, returning a moment later with Wally and little Jimmy. They'd obviously been told the news and had come to say their goodbyes to Rusty. Father and son stood in the doorway, Jimmy glued to Wally's side, small hand gripped in the larger one. His dark eyes were wide and frightened, but the boy bravely extricated himself from his father's grasp and walked to his pet's side.

Callie, for all the control she'd been able to muster to remain detached during Drew's treatment of the animal, could not watch this final admission of defeat, the grieving for a beloved pet.

She stepped outside into the cool night air, wrapping her arms about herself. Drew joined her a few minutes later. She asked no questions, and they stood in silence. Though not much past ten-thirty Main Street was deserted, quiet as a ghost town.

"I helped Jimmy pick out that pup five months ago," Drew said finally. "Wally'd thought to get himself a hunting dog and a pet for his son at the same time." He stared up at the stars, hands jammed in his pockets. "Told me it was time the boy learned how to handle responsibility for another."

Drew blinked slowly, head still tipped back on his neck. "Well, Jimmy's handling it, for a seven-year-old boy. Hell of a way for a kid to learn responsibility, though."

Despite her efforts, Callie felt a tear slip down her cheek. She grieved for the boy and his pet, and she grieved for Drew, too. This was not why he had become a veterinarian and built a clinic. Not to lose half-grown pups and watch a little boy's initial experience with death.

She sniffed, and felt Drew's hand seek hers. She wished she'd thought to make the comforting gesture first, but now that he had, she held nothing back as she gripped his fingers tightly. The strength and comfort flowed between them, in both directions.

"I'm sorry, Drew," she whispered. "I wish I could have helped."

He sighed, dropping his chin to his chest. "I'm glad for what you did. And I'm sorry I snapped at you. But I've been trained to handle situations like this, whereas you . . ."

"I know my performance up to this point may contradict me, but I can keep a stiff upper lip when I need to, Drew," Callie said softly. "I hope you know that. And I don't care how well-trained anyone is, I don't think it's ever easy to see a creature suffer.''

"No, even years of training doesn't lessen it." He rubbed his free hand over his face. "You'd make a good vet, Callie, if the notion ever took you. You've got the love and the desire to provide comfort and support.''

"I'd hate to put you out of a job, though," she said, trying for a lighter tone.

He gave a faint chuckle. "Unlike Dodge City, I think this town would be big enough for the both of us." He lifted one shoulder.

"Ah, well. I can't save every patient. I never expected to, only to do my best. But I didn't want you to see me fail, Callie," he murmured.

Her mouth dropped open, but she quickly closed it. Even in the dim light, she could see a faint flush creep across his cheeks. She'd almost said he didn't need to impress her, but she realized that was not the point. She'd grown up with two men whose pride was much like that of the one who stood beside her now. It was the protectiveness in them that spurred such an aim. They needed the women they cared for to know they could count on their men. They defined who they were by such criteria. Such a perspective in the city would seem overbearing and chauvinistic. Here, though, it was fitting, and often a matter of survival.

Callie wondered what solace to offer Drew but could think of nothing that would help. It was hard to fail, no matter the reason. Hadn't she confessed as much to Drew as he comforted her during the thunderstorm? Like her, he wasn't looking for words of sympathy. Understanding, though, she could provide. A simple *you're not alone* might be all he needed.

"You're like me, Drew," she said tenderly. "You want things badly, and because you care so much it hurts that much worse when you don't get them. But don't stop wanting.''

"I would, you know, if I knew how. But I don't." He squeezed her hand. "Anyway, thanks again.''

"I just wish I could have done more," she said.

"You did what you could." He turned his head toward her, and she saw that his eyes had lost their bleak look, though they had changed—infinitesimally but significantly—as he gazed back at her. "I meant thanks for being here now, when I need a friend more than a trained assistant."

She squeezed back, unable to speak. Yes, she was Drew's friend, and he needed her. Though she might wish for more, right now she felt grateful it seemed enough.

Chapter Eight

Though they had discussed it, Callie still found it hard to realize that Maura Foster would be the one to run the Farrell Family Inn this summer.

At the first meeting of the B&B subcommittee at Callie's house, she had mentioned to Maura her need for an interim proprietor and had been inundated by Maura's questions, overcome by her enthusiasm. Callie had tried to remain cautious, telling Maura that she was looking at other candidates, but Callie realized quickly that Maura was perfect for the job.

It was impossible not to like Maura. When Callie explained she hadn't found a spare moment to buy curtains for the bedrooms, Maura volunteered to run some up on her own sewing machine. "It'd only take a few minutes, honestly! I could do some with tiebacks, some with café curtains and valances. Oh, and wouldn't it be pretty to cross-stitch a border around the edges?"

When Callie mentioned she'd been hoping to find some quilts made by local folk, Maura knew just who to talk to. "Flossie Campbell makes the most beautiful quilts in nearly every pattern! She'd probably make them to order in colors to match the rooms." But here Maura looked momentarily dubious. "I'm afraid she might charge a lot for one. A hundred dollars or more." Callie assured her the price could be managed, as Drew and Hank contributed their opinions and suggestions, too.

However, it was when Maura dropped to her knees to pet Hannah in a spontaneous gesture, laughing as the spaniel licked her face, and became absolutely enthralled by the news of Pavlova's pregnancy, that Callie knew she was lost. From that moment, she stopped talking about "if" Maura took the position and started talking about "when."

After the men left, the two women moved from room to room and Callie explained what still needed to be done and what the end result would be. It was eminently satisfying to converse with someone nearly as enthusiastic about the inn as Callie herself was, someone who could appreciate the amount of thought and the level of detail she had put into the project. And Callie realized with a start that she was conferring on Maura more than a position. She was, in a sense, giving Maura her home, and for a while this would be Maura's place.

And with that thought, Callie knew that that was how it must be. If the inn were to succeed, guests must recognize they were coming into a well-loved home. Maura could convey that feeling, but in doing so, Callie would have to relinquish her family's home to the other woman.

"It'll only be for three months," she felt compelled to warn Maura again, "until Mom and Dad can return and run the inn themselves."

Maura wasn't fazed. She ran her hand over the newly stripped woodwork in the living room and smiled. "That's all right," she said. "By then, maybe I'll have a home of my own." She threw Callie an abashed look. "I've been renting ever since Wayne died, you know. Our house—I had to sell it to pay bills. Apartment living isn't...*living*, if you know what I mean."

With this opening, Callie still could not make herself ask the questions she so wanted to. *And in three months? Do you have plans then, plans with Drew?* Seeing the two of them together gave her no clues. Drew's attitude toward Maura was much as his toward Callie, though perhaps he didn't treat Maura quite so familiarly as he did Callie. But then, wouldn't a man be less familiar with his near fiancée than with his honorary sister?

Perhaps Maura and Drew weren't such a sure thing as Nate implied, Callie mused. She had certainly heard nothing in town to refute or confirm the rumor. But Nate and Drew were best friends. If anyone would know what was going on with Drew, it'd be Nate.

It shouldn't matter either way, Callie reminded herself. What Drew and Maura felt for each other was their business. Yet Callie became quite cold, as if drenched by icy water, as images pressed in on her—of Maura in her inn barely a half mile from Drew in his house, or worse, both of them in either one.

Her distraction from these thoughts, ironically, was Maura. Callie's heart went out to her as, just before the other woman left, Maura turned to her new employer and asked, "About Davey? My son?" Her gaze dropped to her fingers curled around the doorknob, as if she found the matter hard to bring up, though she knew she must. "I hope it won't bother you to have a child live here. He's a quiet boy, maybe too quiet, and he won't get into mischief, I promise you. And he can sleep in my room. Wayne's mother has a rollaway I can borrow." Maura smiled her sweet smile. "Though it's exactly like a regular bed, Davey finds sleeping on a rollaway quite an adventure. It's the wheels on it, I guess."

Callie smiled back, leaning against the doorjamb. "I don't see any problem with that arrangement."

"You're sure?"

"Sure I'm sure. Davey can even help out if he likes. There are chickens to feed and weeds to pull—if he can tell the difference between weeds and flowers. How old is Davey, anyway?''

"He's four. He'll be five in October."

"Hannah loves four-, almost five-year-olds." Callie glanced down at the dog underfoot. "Don't you, Hannah?"

"Hopefully not for breakfast," Maura said with simulated ambivalence, eyeing Hannah's barrellike trunk dubiously.

The two women laughed. Maura stooped to place an unhygienic kiss on Hannah's black, shiny nose. "Madam, your reputation precedes you, I'm afraid."

And as Maura bid a lighthearted goodbye, Callie realized who'd likely entertained Maura with stories of Hannah the Hulk.

Callie and Hank Peterson sat enjoying a late-afternoon glass of iced tea on the front porch when Drew pulled in the drive.

Callie pushed the limp straggles of hair behind her ears and wondered what she must look like. She'd grown somewhat complacent in the week that had passed since the episode in Drew's clinic. Drew had sprung more than one of his unannounced visits on her, and, surprisingly, her heart no longer hammered—or at least not with a deafening din—at the crunch of gravel on the driveway.

Determined it would not do so now, she concentrated on making herself shrug philosophically—she probably looked like she'd been working hard, which she had. Hank had been sawing, drilling and pounding for hours up in the west bedroom's closet, while she wrestled with tearing up the carpet runner in the front hall. That had taken the good part of two hours, with Hank occasionally coming down to shake a gray head and murmur a multitude of "Mercy, Callie's" as he beheld her progress.

When finally he had started running the electric sander up and down the wood floor she'd uncovered, Callie had been tempted simply to stand back and watch Hank's smooth, precise and economical movements. But she'd needed to continue the distasteful process of stripping woodwork.

Now, she wished heartily that the day had been less jam-packed as she rubbed her tired shoulders. She immediately regretted the wave she returned in response to Drew's as a painful twinge shot through her muscles. Wincing, Callie worked her shoulder in a full range of motion. Tomorrow would be a furniture-hunting day, she decided.

"Evenin', Doc," Hank said.

"Evening, Hank, Callie." Drew mounted the steps and dropped a large straw basket in her lap. "Happy May Day," he said with a smile, taking a seat on the porch rail while Hannah pushed a wet nose between his knees.

"May Day!" Callie's eyes widened in surprised delight, her aches momentarily forgotten. "Oh, Drew, I didn't think anybody remembered May Day anymore."

She dug excitedly through the basket of goodies, holding up and identifying each gift with glee. "Wild asparagus! So you're the one who's been raiding all my secret patches!" She glared at him.

"You're the one who showed me where they all were," Drew pointed out, scratching Hannah behind the ears and making her groan with pleasure.

"I was seven years old and you threatened to tell my mother I'd ridden my bike out past the railroad tracks if I didn't."

"We all make our choices," he informed her with equanimity.

"And a bouquet of lilacs!" she cried, ignoring him. Callie plunged her face into the redolent blooms. "I *love* how these smell." She set them gently to the side and picked up a Mason jar. "Mmm—homemade piccalilli. My friends in L.A. think I'm crazy when I rave about homemade picca-lilli."

She held up a shiny brown nut and shot Drew a quizzical glance. "A buckeye?"

"Everyone needs a lucky buckeye."

"You two have buckeye collections when you were young 'uns?" Hank asked.

"Did we!" Callie said. "Nate and I were the envy of all the kids because we had a buckeye tree in our front yard, and every fall we'd have more buckeyes than anyone." She extracted another jar from the basket on her lap. "And mulberries," she breathed. "Heavens, but I love mulberries."

"I remember one time you didn't," Drew reminisced. "You were about five and you kept tailing Nate and me like a puppy wherever we went, so we found a mulberry tree and held you down and smeared mulberry juice all over your legs and arms and face." He laughed. "You screamed and kicked like a wild Indian."

"I *looked* like a wild Indian," Callie reminded him, laughing herself. "I never had so many baths in a week, from Mom trying to scrub the stain off."

Drew grinned in a years-too-late apology and Callie gave him a reproving glance, suddenly feeling more lighthearted than she had in weeks. How much easier, she thought with a twinge of regret but with undeniable relief, to associate with Drew this way, rather than with her heart in her throat. Perhaps familiarity actually bred content, and there was a chance she'd grow used to Drew's role in her life as friend and neighbor. How else could she smile at him with genuine appreciation, so easily, so naturally, before continuing to catalog the contents of her basket?

"Mmm, fresh rhubarb. Mom's got the best recipe for rhubarb sauce. And don't tell me—oh, Drew, your mother's elderberry jam!" Callie lifted the squat jar of jeweled jelly to her lips and pressed them reverently to it. "Alice Barnett makes the best elderberry jam in the county," she informed Hank.

"And your mother makes the best apple butter," Drew said with a none-too-subtle hint.

Callie began loading her presents back into the basket. "A fair trade. I think Mom put by several jars of it in the cellar."

She rose and glanced from Drew to Hank. She indicated the front door with a tilt of her head. "Why don't you both come on in while I dig it out?" she suggested in a surge of neighborliness. "And stay for supper while you're at it." Surely *that* would put to rest any question in her mind that she could adjust to Drew's presence.

"Don't mind if I do," Drew said.

Hank pulled his elderly body from his chair. "Sounds like a plan to me."

An hour later the three of them sat down to Callie's pot roast and more of the same good, easy conversation.

Yes, Callie decided, she'd accommodated. She was becoming comfortable with the role Drew played in her life. And yet she couldn't deny he would always be special to her, as she watched him speak animatedly to her and Hank about the calls he'd made to surrounding farms and communities, tending livestock and animals of every description. In turn he questioned her about her progress on the house, and she found herself going on about it quite easily. They discussed the subcommittee, how their informal classes in inn management, held at the town hall, were being well attended.

And as she met Drew's gaze across the supper table again and again with that comfort, Callie was convinced what she felt for him was merely the sibling affection he felt for her.

When they were finished eating, Hank rose with apologies for eating and running, mysteriously informing them he had "a few things to attend to."

"Like the Widda Lawsen," Drew murmured conspiratorially when Hank had left.

Callie's eyes widened. "Cora?"

"They've been seen holding hands under the table at Myra's Maid Rite. And Hank's wafted past more than one person in a cloud of Aqua Velva."

"Really?" Callie laughed. "Hank?"

"Documentable," Drew insisted. "I have excellent sources."

They both chuckled before the laughter died on Callie's lips in the rapidly darkening room. Dusk had settled as they ate, and twilight was fast approaching. She rose and began briskly clearing the table, waving away Drew's efforts to help.

"You don't need to stick around either," she said in what only Nate or her father would have recognized as Sally Farrell's most no-nonsense tone, as she stacked dishes next to the sink and began running hot water into it.

Drew, however, grabbed a towel and began drying the dishes as she washed and rinsed them.

She glanced at him sternly. "I thought I said you didn't need to hang around."

"Mind if I do, just for the hell of it?" Drew asked softly.

She slid a soapy dishcloth over a submerged plate. The sudden disturbance his tone produced was there, but manageable. "No, of course not," Callie replied.

They worked along, side by side, both lost in thought, until everything was washed, dried and put away. Callie ran her damp hands down the front of her jeans and glanced at Drew, who was folding the dish towel and hanging it up.

"Why don't we sit outside?" he suggested.

Callie hesitated, but only for a moment. She had gotten into the habit of relaxing out there in the evening after a hard day's work and she looked forward to it. No reason to deny herself tonight, just because of Drew's presence.

"I'll grab a sweater," she said.

An old ratty one of her mother's hung on a hook by the back door, and she slid it over her shoulders as he followed her through the house to the front door. They settled on the wood swing on the side porch and looked out toward Drew's house across the field.

The evening was exceptionally clear, and the fireflies, harbingers of the warm, early summer to come, had just begun their tentative on-off courtship ritual. Crickets and frogs competed noisily for top billing at the creek side. The stars had no such contest as they appeared one by one, until the more prominent constellations had taken their rightful place at center stage in the sky.

Callie wrapped her sweater more tightly about her and took a deep breath. "Gosh, the air smells so fresh!" She exhaled noisily. "Some days, the smog in Los Angeles is so thick I can taste it—a dirty, metallic taste that burns the eyes and nose. Here," she sniffed luxuriously, "it's nothing but clean, pure—" she sniffed suspiciously "—and sometimes manure-scented air."

Drew laughed softly, his teeth gleaming in the twilight. "Anderson's hog complex."

"I don't care, I still love it." She stretched her arms over her head and groaned suddenly.

"What's wrong?" Drew asked.

She massaged her shoulders painfully. "I guess I overdid it today." She half smiled, half grimaced. "I was a wood-stripping fiend."

"Here." He pushed her hands away and took over, his fingers sure and strong on her aching muscles.

Callie couldn't prevent herself from stiffening. A neighborly dinner and chat was one thing. Touching was quite another.

"You *are* tense," Drew murmured. "You've got a knot here hard as a brick. Here." He turned her so that he had better leverage. "Let your head drop forward. That's it."

It would have taken a better woman than Callie not to respond. Slowly but surely she felt the tension leave her shoulders. "Mmm. That feels like heaven."

Drew was thorough, and when he finished she slumped limply against the cushioned back of the swing with a yawned thanks. In the recesses of her rapidly disintegrating consciousness, she realized the back of her head lay on Drew's outstretched arm and that perhaps she should remove herself to the other side of the swing.

But she felt so tired, so comfortable, after a month of roiling emotions.

They swung gently back and forth for several minutes.

"You shouldn't work so hard, Callie." Drew's voice was low but clear. "You'll hurt yourself, and then what good will you be to your family?"

"Oh, you and Nate," she said with a sleepy smile. "I know you worry, but I'll be fine."

"I do worry. You're so intent. It makes me think that despite your protests you'll be pretty sad to leave this place when the time comes to go back to California."

"I'll be back," was Callie's drowsy reply. She yawned hugely, bringing tears to her eyes. "Once a year, like always."

"Yes. You always come back."

Silence flowered between them. Callie drifted. It felt so cozy to sit there, the coolness of the evening diminished by the warmth emanating from the man beside her, creating a delicious combination of sensations. She felt secure.

"Are you happy right now, Callie?" Drew asked, lullaby quiet.

She nodded, her temple against his cotton shirtsleeve.

"You seem so," he went on, almost to himself. "When I've pictured you, over the years, I've pictured you competent, energetic. Purposeful in the full-speed-ahead way you have of being purposeful." He paused, his breath ruffling her hair. "But I didn't see you happy, and I wondered what would make you so. And now I'm thinking that if it's just a good day's work, a basket of homemade memories and a place to watch the stars on a cool, clear night..."

His voice trailed off and Drew sighed so deeply Callie felt its rumble vibrate to his arm against her cheek. Then he said softly, "What would it take to keep you just as you are right now?"

Disturbed by his tone, Callie's eyes fluttered open at last. In Drew's eyes she saw his concern for her, felt his protective affection, which formed a circle of security around her. "I don't know," she said in answer to his question. And she didn't know, not really, what would make her happy. Or perhaps she knew but, realizing it was unattainable, her heart searched for another kind of happiness that as yet eluded it.

She gazed up at him. He cared for her, and though that care might not inspire desire in him, still it was strong and sure and true.

But in her it inspired...something, an ache for something more, even when she knew there could never be anything more between her and Drew. Even now, the closeness that she'd allowed him as friend and neighbor would not keep its place, but wandered, seemingly without design, into the deepest corners of her heart, distracting it from its purpose.

She had to stop thinking of him that way. She had to stop doing this to herself.

Callie sat up, pressing her hand to his chest and moving away, seeking both physical and emotional distance. "I'm sorry, Drew. I must have dozed for a minute." She pushed her hair back from her face and gave him an apologetic smile. "I guess I'd better drag myself inside and crawl upstairs to bed. Otherwise I'll have to be tossed up through my bedroom window, like a bale of hay through a hay mow." Her lashes fluttered downward as she avoided his probing glance.

"I'm an old hand at baling hay." His voice held that old teasing note, his quiet speculations of a moment ago seemingly forgotten.

She rose, not answering him. "Thanks again for the May basket. It was sweet of you." She yawned again in spite of herself.

"You remember the rest of the ritual, don't you?" Drew stood also. "You're supposed to chase the one who gives you the May basket until you catch him and then you kiss him," he said lightly, still teasing—so it seemed.

She studied the pattern on his shirt, wondering how best to respond. "Like that time when I was nine and still a card-carrying member of the Man Haters' Club?"

Drew chuckled. "I believe your normal reaction to boys was to gag audibly."

"And *you*," she finally looked at him accusingly, now that they were back on the familiar ground of recalling his lifelong torment of her, "chased me clear down to Morton Corner, threatening to plant a big, wet one on me if you did catch me. Like you couldn't have caught me in two steps."

"Ah, the good, old days," he reminisced, catching Callie's fist as she swung it at him playfully. "Well, here's your opportunity to get me back."

Her heart thudded ominously. What was his game? Did he suspect she might feel for him something beyond sisterly affection and want to tease her about it? Why? The vulnerability she'd not felt for several days crept back. He still had such a power to affect her, and she admitted he probably always would. One didn't grow to maturity with another person without developing attachments that no amount of time would ever completely breach.

"I'm in no condition to do any chasing," she answered lightly.

His eyes laughed down at her. "I'm not running."

She schooled her features, trying not to rise to the cool challenge in his eyes. But perhaps this was the perfect opportunity to demonstrate to both Drew and herself that she'd mastered her feelings for him.

Tiptoeing, she leaned toward him, meaning only to give him a light peck, but once she'd started the motion, she realized she could not make this look like the playful gesture she meant to. No, it looked and felt awkward—for she really did feel *something* for Drew. And it would undoubtedly show to her disadvantage.

But she couldn't stop now. Callie intended to give him a sopping smack, as big and wet as the one he'd threatened her with long ago, on his cheek, but Drew turned his head at the last instant. And her puckered lips met his.

They were warm. And soft, and bristly around the edges from the shadow of his day-old beard. As her mouth pressed firmly to his, even though the contact was as innocuous as kisses she gave an elderly relative, something fairly shouted at her that it wasn't the same. Her eyes met his crookedly and she squeezed her lids shut rather than face whatever might be reflected in his gaze. No other part of their bodies touched. There was no time.

"Mwah!" she exclaimed in a parody of those childish familial kisses, and pulled away. She felt her face begin to redden, but her sense of humor finally came to her rescue as she started to laugh at the absurdity of the whole situation. How had he talked her into standing on her front porch and kissing him in years-old retaliation? He really did derive an inordinate amount of pleasure from teasing her!

"Well?" she asked.

"Please don't gag," Drew begged over his own laughter, as if his ego couldn't bear that assault on it. A trick of light seemed to make his eyes blue flames as he looked down at her.

"But how will I ever face my fellow Man-Hater members if I don't?" Her pulse thundered in her ears and her fingers itched desperately to go to her lips.

"That's your problem. And I'll take that as my cue to leave—if you can manage not to stick your finger down your throat until I get out of the driveway."

"Then you'd better hurry," she quipped more easily than she'd have thought possible at that moment, given the jittery feeling that had come over her all of a sudden.

"I'm on my way," Drew said. "Thanks for dinner."

"Don't forget your apple butter." Callie indicated the jar that sat on the porch step where she had placed it earlier that evening.

Drew obligingly picked up the jar, took the porch steps two at a time and was halfway to his Bronco when he turned. "Say, you want to go fishing tomorrow morning?" he called.

"Fishing?" Callie repeated.

"You know—poles, line, rods, reels. Fish, even, if we're lucky."

"I don't know, Drew." She'd be crazy to solicit anymore contact with him than necessary. "Sounds pretty challenging."

"I promise I'll bait your hook and clean anything you catch worth saving," he coaxed. In the glow of the porch light she could see him rubbing the jar of apple butter with his thumb.

She was tempted to say yes. "No, I meant like casting and reeling—stuff that aching arm muscles would find difficult."

Drew smiled. "I guarantee you'll just have to sit—real still, mind you—"

"I have so much work to do—"

"I'll have you back by nine."

"I've never been fishing before—"

"You haven't? Then you've got to go!" He slid a hand into one hip pocket. "I don't ask just anybody to my private fishing spot," he offered, as if that made a difference.

Callie smiled and turned her head against one shoulder. Somehow, it did make a difference.

"So I just sit still, huh?"

"Uh-huh."

"Like sleeping still?"

"Stiller," he whispered.

Callie caved in, wondering why she was doing so—except that the impact of the past few minutes was receding and her comfort level was returning. And now, Drew's invitation to fish struck her as the height of platonic fraternization.

"Sounds like my kind of sport. Okay, I'll go fishing."

"Good." Drew tossed the jar a foot in the air and caught it deftly. "I'll pick you up at five. Dress warm."

"Sure, five o'clock," she called gamely. He was kidding her again, of course. She pressed her fingertips to her lips, almost as a reminder. Then, yawning again, she turned and called Hannah before going inside.

Chapter Nine

Something was disturbing Callie's sleep. Something as persistent as the buzz of a mosquito, as annoying as the whine of a lawn mower on a Saturday morning. Something as grating to the senses as the intermittent ring of a phone. The phone!

She fell out of her low bed onto Hannah. After untangling her limbs, Callie stumbled toward the door of the darkened bedroom, stubbing her toe on the corner of the dresser.

"Ow-ow-*ow*," she chanted as her eyes blearily located the small table in the hallway that held the offending instrument. She snatched it up mid-ring. "Why are you calling me so *early?*" she demanded, her voice husky with sleep, and promptly hung up.

She was halfway to her bedroom when the ringing began again. Callie groaned and staggered back to the table, fumbled for the phone. "*What?* What do you want?" she groaned. She wedged the receiver between her shoulder and cheek and rubbed her eyes wearily.

"Good morning, Callie," a deep voice responded to her rude greeting.

"Drew? Is that you?" Her sleep-muddled mind began to clear. "Good grief, what time is it?"

His chuckle coming over the telephone line did nothing for her disposition. "I thought you might need a wake-up call and a little time to get yourself together before I picked you up. I did mention last night when I'd be by this morning, didn't I? Five o'clock?"

"Fi—!" Callie's drowsy voice rose and cracked. "Five o'clock? I thought you were kidding! Drew, *nobody* gets up at this hour of the morning!"

"Fish do."

"Then fish have the brains of . . . fish." She pushed back her mussed hair with her hand, then stuck it under her arm. It was *cold* at five o'clock in the morning.

"The easier to catch them with," Drew supplied. "You sure you'll still want to go, once you've forgiven me for getting you up at this ungodly hour?" His voice softened. "I wouldn't have asked you, you know, if I didn't think it was worth it."

"It better be." Callie yawned. "Well, I'm up, so you might as well come get me. I won't guarantee what condition I'll be in."

"I'll take my chances." Drew laughed.

Callie was dressed in snug jeans and waffle-soled boots, with a warm sweater under her down vest, when Drew pulled up. He leaned an elbow on the window jamb and eyed her attire speculatively. "You sure you want to wear that jacket?" he asked.

She glanced down at her pastel-colored, down-covered chest. "It's the warmest thing I have."

"Well, I'd hate to see it get dirty. Here," he turned and fished in the back seat of the Bronco, "why don't you go put that away and wear this?" He produced a large, warm-looking army jacket that had seen better days. "You'll be okay in this."

"If I don't get lost in it first," she muttered as she slipped into the jacket and rolled up the sleeves six inches. She returned the vest to the house and left a note on the door where Hank could find it.

"Ready?" Drew asked.

"As I'll ever be," Callie said dubiously. She climbed in the front seat of the Bronco and noticed the hopeful bump of black fur planted next to the door. She glanced across at Drew, just as hopeful.

He nodded. "Sure, bring her along."

Hannah scrambled with zest between the two of them and panted happily. Drew turned to back out of the driveway and caught Callie's eye. "You'll love it. Trust me."

The sun had not yet appeared when they reached the creek, but rays scouting over the horizon lighted Drew and Callie's way to the sheltered bank. He backed the Bronco to a smooth patch of land, and they started unloading. Callie was charged with carrying a round foam container closer to the bank while Drew carried a larger cooler and the fishing equipment.

She set down her armload and puffed her hair out of her face. "Now what?" She pulled the voluminous jacket tighter around herself and wondered how Drew could walk about in this chill in just a flannel shirt and jeans. He looked as if he rose regularly at this time of the morning and actually liked it.

"First," Drew squatted and opened the metal tackle box, pulling out a coil of line, "I need to set my line out on the other side of that log." He pointed to a section of bracken under a large black willow that drooped over the deepest part of the creek. "If I don't get it in the water first thing, it could be hours before I get a bite."

"What about me?"

"You," he skillfully tied a hook on the line, "have a mission."

"A mission?"

"To catch breakfast." He smiled over at her.

"But what are you doing, then?" As Drew flipped the bait bucket open, she pushed the inquisitive Hannah away and crouched beside him with interest. He produced an old margarine container.

"This is to catch dinner and to show up that cocky brother of yours." He pried the lid off the container and Callie's nose was assailed by the most noxious odor she'd ever smelled. She sat back quickly and grabbed Hannah's collar to prevent the dog's plunging her muzzle into the foul-smelling stuff that Drew held with a sort of proud reverence.

"My God, Drew, wh—" She blew two gusts of air through her nostrils, trying to eradicate that horrible smell. "What *is* that?"

"It's my special recipe for catfish bait," he answered, apparently oblivious to the repulsive reek emanating from the margarine tub. "Generically known as 'stink bait.'"

"How apt. What's in it?"

He glanced at her dubiously, as if wondering whether she really wanted to know. "Cornmeal, flour and, ah . . . a little animal blood—"

"Animal blood?" Had she had anything in her stomach, it would have risen in barely contained outrage. A little worm was one thing, but Drew wouldn't catch her putting anything that had thought that mixture palatable in her mouth.

"Mmm-hmm. And a few other things." Drew had pinched a dollop of the dark red-brown concoction between two fingers and mercifully snapped the lid back on the container. He concentrated on molding the claylike mixture onto his hook.

Callie wondered what could be more revolting than animal blood, but she had a perverse need to know what "other things" Drew had added to his bait. "What else is in there?"

He merely shook his head as he rose and angled his way onto the tip of the log and dropped the line in, securing it on a strong, thick branch. He squatted and washed his hands in the creek. "It's a secret. And if I told you, you'd tell Nate.

I'm trying to give him a run for his money. He said he caught a fifteen-pound catfish here last week. He *said*." He made his way carefully back to Callie and Hannah. "We'll see."

"I'm not after any fifteen-pound catfish, am I?" she asked nervously, aware that a hefty cat, much less a cat-*fish*, weighed less than that.

"Nope." He picked up a modern-looking fishing pole and selected a hook to rig to its line. He extracted a small, wriggling earthworm from the bait bucket. "Just some little sunfish that we can fry up." He glanced over at her. "Want me to bait your hook for you?"

Callie scooted closer to him. "Just the first time," she said staunchly. She wanted to do her part. "Then I'll know how to do it."

"That's my girl," Drew approved. She watched as he deftly threaded the rod's hook through the worm with a surgeon's precision. She knew her efforts wouldn't be quite that neat.

He got her set up on the bank with her pole, Hannah cuddled next to her. Then Drew started a fire and set an old metal coffeepot over it, unaware of her eyes on him as he went to check his line briefly, before coming back to the fire and unpacking the rest of the gear.

"Do you come here a lot?" Callie called over her shoulder as she huddled on the damp ground.

"Shh," he warned. "I thought I told you this was very still work. Remember?"

"Oh." She was silent for a moment, her breath puffing around her, and then she whispered loudly, "Do you?"

Drew chuckled. "Yeah. This is one of Nate's and my favorite spots. Usually we fish in the river early in the day. It's better for morning fishing, the creek for evening. With the new lake, there'll be a slew of new sites to fish. I'm pretty partial to this place, though."

"You are?" Her lower lip grew as she frowned in thought. "Why haven't you ever asked me to come here before?" she asked, pretending sulkiness. "I mean, I showed you all my wild asparagus patches."

"Be honest now." He blew on the fire and it flared against the gust. "Would you have wanted to get up before the sun and trek out here in the damp and cold when you were a girl?"

Her heart skipped a little at his use of the past tense. "You never seemed to have an aversion to making me thoroughly damp and cold by dunking me at Miller's swimming hole," she pointed out innocently. "What's so different about this place?"

"Not a thing, come to think of it." Drew took a step toward her, and she scooted away from him, giggling.

"Stop right there, Drew Barnett." She held up one hand and brandished the fishing pole in the other. "I'm on a mission," she said importantly. "Remember?"

"If you keep thrashing the pole around like that, the only thing you'll catch is the seat of your pants." He scowled at her unconvincingly. "Now pipe down and enjoy the dawn."

And a gorgeous dawn it was turning out to be, Callie thought as she sat up straighter, both hands tucked into the cuffs of the overlarge jacket, one of them holding the pole. She was finally awake enough to take an interest in the spot Drew had brought her to.

The sun was turning the sky a violet blue as it pressed up over the horizon. Shafts of light glanced gently off the smooth eddies and currents carrying the murky water south. In the west, the moon, still not willing to relinquish the sky, hung as large and luminous as an opal, a mosaic of purplish grays and golden greens. The trees on either bank became more definitely green by the minute, slowly coming alive with birds and insects. Callie heard a robin's distinct *cheeri-up, cheeri-up* as well as the musical call of the meadowlark. It was peaceful and fraught with activity all at once, she thought.

She sighed deeply. "This *is* nice," she murmured as Drew came up behind her and handed her a steaming mug of coffee. Hannah grunted as he gave her a shove and knelt next to Callie, repositioning her pole a little higher. "I'm glad you asked me to come with you this morning," she said sincerely.

"Good. I didn't think you'd feel that way for a while." Drew sipped his coffee. "You've truly never been fishing before?"

"Nope. Nate put up with dragging me nearly every place else, but he put down his foot when it came to fishing, and Dad agreed." She threw him a sardonic look. "One of those male rituals, I'm sure. Mysterious concoctions and secret places."

"A woman wouldn't understand," Drew concurred.

She chuckled and kept her pole-holding hand steady as she raised the cup Drew had given her to her lips. "Sorry I was such a grouch earlier. I'm not an early riser, and even when I do get up I'm not always pleasant first off. Everyone in my family has learned to keep their distance."

"Mmm. Well, it's frightening. I'd hate to wake up to that sort of abuse every day."

Callie shot him a sidelong glance, wondering at the seemingly innocent remark. "It has its advantages," she said. "Nate long ago decided it was easier to do the morning chores himself than try to rouse me to help him." She grinned.

Drew grinned back. "Brat." He rumpled her already rumpled hair and rose. "I better check that line."

He was the furthest he could be from her when she got a bite. She dropped her coffee with a yelp and stood, clamping both hands on the pole. "Drew! I've got something!"

"Well, hold on a sec." He was bent over his own line and she heard his soft, "Damn, a carp." He swiftly pulled out the hook and dropped the fish back into the water with a splash. "Use the reel, Callie."

She unlocked the reel and spun it in jerky revolutions until her catch cleared the water. A five-inch crappie wriggled pitifully on the end of Callie's line.

He strode over and grabbed the line, then the crappie. "I'm surprised you could feel this on the end of your line," he grunted and extracted her hook from the fish's upper lip. He tossed it back in the creek with what Callie thought was immense unconcern.

"Hey," she protested, "that's my breakfast!"

"No, it's not." Drew pulled another earthworm from the bait bucket and handed it to her. "Too small."

"What was wrong with the one you caught?"

"Carp," he offered succinctly, dipping into his special concoction and rebaiting his own hook.

"Oh." Even she knew no self-respecting angler would dream of eating carp. Still, Callie couldn't help muttering as she concentrated on baiting her hook, "We'll *never* get anything to eat if you keep tossing back everything we pull out."

"Patience, girl," Drew coaxed in his smoky voice. "Patience."

Realizing she was quite out of her element, she refrained from further comment. It wasn't long before she caught a decent-sized sunfish, followed by three more. Drew filleted them on a Plexiglas cutting board set on top of the larger cooler, and soon the sounds and smells of frying fish and farm-fresh eggs filled the small clearing.

Her "mission" completed, Callie sat to one side of the fire, she and Hannah watching avidly as Drew expertly turned the cornmeal-coated fish in the large frying pan. The combination of early morning activity and fresh air had made her ravenous. She shrugged her slightly sore shoulders in contentment. The damp ground was making itself known through the seat of her jeans, she smelled distinctly fishy, and she definitely had some grit beneath her fingernails. Still, she felt marvelous.

She was unaware how warm her unconscious smile was until Drew glanced over at her and gave her one of his own. He's very much in command today, she thought, completely in his element, doing what he loves and can do best. If he meant to endear himself to her, or at least allay any awkwardness, he had certainly picked an unconventional but successful method.

She realized she was having a wonderful time, mostly because of the congenial atmosphere that had sprung up between Drew and herself. The disturbing sensations of last night's encounter faded and the ache that had threatened in her chest subsided and was replaced by that same security that had wrapped about her like a child's favorite and most familiar blanket.

"Do me a favor, would you?" Drew broke through her euphoria. "Go check my line and then fetch the napkins off the dash of the Bronco, please."

"Why do you have to keep checking it?" Callie asked as she did so.

"Sometimes catfish will take the bait and then they just sit on the bottom with it. They don't always nab it and try to swim away."

"Now why do you think they do that?" she asked, puzzled.

Drew chuckled. "If I knew how a catfish thought, Callie, I'd be giving that brother of yours a run for his money, that's for sure."

Callie continued to the Bronco, deep in thought. She'd never pondered fish psychology before, and she was intrigued. She might have caught her first fish, but she knew the nuances of angling would take her years to learn.

Is that what she wanted, to learn the ins and outs of fishing, the whys and hows, over the years? To enjoy more mornings like these, or more evenings like the previous night? With Drew?

If only she could. She'd give anything to preserve this moment, these feelings, forever. She wondered what Drew would say if she were to turn, spreading her arms, and say, *This. This is what makes me happy.*

"Hurry up with the napkins," he called as he forked fish and eggs onto two plates.

Callie hurried, and caught a glimpse of herself in the rear view mirror as she grabbed the napkins off the dashboard.

"Oh!" Her breath left her and then she burst out laughing. She backed out of the truck. "Drew Barnett, why didn't you tell me I looked like this all morning?"

Drew was already digging into the moist, hot fish. "Like what? You look fine." He took a gulp of coffee as he watched her walk to the fire and flop down on the other side of it.

"Fine?" She lifted a hank of hair away from her ear and dropped it again. "I look like I combed my hair with an eggbeater, and you could send distress signals with a blanket and the shine off my nose."

"What's the matter?" he chuckled. "Can't believe you were having such a good time without your powder puff?" He raised a forkful of fish to his mouth and chewed thoughtfully while perusing her. "I think you look natural this way," he complimented her. "I don't know why women wear makeup at all."

"Spoken like a true...man."

"It's just my opinion, but you look so much better without it. Most women do. Fish good?"

"Mmm-hmm." She forgot her looks and began to enjoy the taste of fresh fish on her tongue. "Actually, I honestly don't think I look all that bad au naturel," she said after a minute. "I guess six years in L.A., where most men prefer their women dressed to the nines every minute of the day, has made me think that's the norm."

"If any of what I've read about California is true, I tend to believe most of what goes on there is *not* the norm."

Callie had no reply to Drew's rather emphatically uttered statement. Why would he feel so strongly about whatever the attitudes Californians exhibited? Except that, for some reason, Drew seemed intent on showing her the riches that could be had in Iowa, hidden in the simple routine of fishing in a creek.

His next words reinforced that realization. "Besides, what could be better than just enjoying a beautiful morning like this, talking and joking like we don't have a care in the world?"

"Nothing, of course," she said warily. The atmosphere between them had changed. They *had* been acting like youngsters, carefree and easy. Now, though, Drew seemed somewhat annoyed, although she sensed it wasn't at her, but at himself.

She watched Drew take a last bite and set his plate aside, whistling for Hannah to clean it off, as he leaned back on his elbows, ankles crossed. At his call, the spaniel bounded out of the brush, sodden to the belly. In two lumbering leaps, the dog plowed across Drew's chest, soaking its flannel width.

"Hannah!" Callie burst out and clapped a hand over her mouth as, for the second time that morning, laughter assailed her.

The mood reverted to its earlier easy state. Drew was perfect, raising his palms in a *Why me?* pose as Hannah, oblivious to the mess she'd caused, swept her tongue across the metal plate, her tags clinking a tinny chime, her soggy hind end swishing against Drew's shirtsleeve. He stood and with exaggerated dignity began brushing bits of muddy grass and twigs off his front.

"Drew, I'm sorry," Callie offered, not sounding a bit apologetic, as she wiped a tear from the corner of her eye. "I swear, she's such a little barbarian when it comes to food."

"I sense your remorse." Drew shook his head. "But please don't worry about it," he said gallantly. "This shirt has certainly seen worse than a dog's muddy paws."

"You can't be comfortable, though."

"Two minutes by this fire and it'll be dry." And to Callie's chagrin, he began to unbutton his shirt with one hand, pulling its tails free from the waistband of his jeans with the other.

Her mirth deserted her, and she quickly found another place to look as Drew located three yard-long sticks, propped them against each other, and draped his wet shirt like a tepee.

"There. Dry in no time," he pronounced before pouring himself another cup of coffee and settling next to her this time, near the warmest part of the fire.

"You'll freeze," she ventured, very aware of his naked chest.

He took a long swallow of coffee and propped his forearm on his bent knee. "Not with this fire. I'm near sweltering, in fact."

Callie tried to finish her own breakfast, but only two bites made their sluggish way down her throat. It *was* getting warm, she realized, either from the sensations stirring in her or from the blaze, and she slipped the large jacket off. She realized suddenly that, though civilization lay but a few miles away, here the wilderness completely surrounded them. She heard the sounds that meant business hours at the creek bank: little scufflings in the brush as the head of the household foraged for food, the distressing peeps of hungry babies wanting breakfast, a bee droning close by, shopping for nectar. She would have preferred to listen to those sounds forever, without having to think about the sudden tension that had sprung up between Drew and her, almost a product of the untamed environment.

Finally, she gave in to Hannah's not very subtle whimpers and relinquished her plate to the dog's rough tongue. "That was delicious, Drew," she said. "Thanks."

"My pleasure." He leaned back on his elbows again, and she sneaked a look. Drew stared pensively at the center of the fire. His position accentuated the musculature of his chest, arms and stomach. Not an ounce of fat dared blemish his honed hardness. He looked as if he hefted large animals around for a living, which he did. Callie clasped her knees to her chest and tried not to think, while her head and heart throbbed with the nearness of Drew. She searched her mind madly for a way to regain their earlier casual footing.

"I've really enjoyed our fishing expedition, Drew," she said, thinking perhaps, with her mention of California, he thought her too used to sophisticated entertainment to enjoy such a quaint activity. "Stink bait and all. Thank you for bringing me here."

He returned her smile. "You're welcome. Now's the worst part, though. Cleaning up."

"Oh, I'll do that. You did the cooking." Callie started to rise, relieved to put distance between them, but Drew pulled her supporting arm from under her.

She toppled against him with a squeak of surprise.

"It can wait, unless you're in a hurry," he said. He settled all the way back on the ground and wrapped his arms around her.

Her hands braced against the warm skin of his chest as her head reeled. She found herself unable to draw a single satisfying breath. Oh, Lord, what was he up to? Last night had been bad enough, but did he really, truly mean to devil it out of her that she might still . . . still be sweet on him?

And why, *why* would it be so important to him to know?

"Relax, Callie," he said in a low voice. "You're skittish as a new colt."

Her heart thundered and she forced herself to drop her ear against his chest, lest she meet his eyes. His heart beat steadily and reassuringly in her ear.

"Hear anything interesting?" Drew asked softly.

She refused to surrender to the impulse to rub her cheek against the rough sprinkling of hair. He smelled like creek and dog and sweat. She closed her eyes and allowed herself one inhalation of that strangely exhilarating combination. "It's telling me all your secrets," she joked breathlessly. "Treasured fishing spots and recipes for lethal catfish bait."

"I'm discovered." He brushed her hair from her face. "Anything else?"

"I—I don't know." She pretended to listen intently, striving to maintain the light atmosphere. He had to be teasing; there was no other reason for him to act this way. "It's kind of muddled, you're stomach's making so much racket below." She shrugged against him. "Not to worry, though. I've got the information I need to get you ejected from the Male Bonding League." She tried to rise.

But Drew hauled her upward so their faces were very close. "Not before I get you thrown out of the Man Haters' Club," he murmured, and raised his mouth to hers.

She gasped from shock and confusion and the sensation of his lips on hers. *Heavens, what's happening?* How could he be so cruel, so unfeeling, to torment her like this!

She noted, however, that his body didn't feel cruel or unfeeling. His mouth was soft and warm against hers. He grazed his lips across hers, urging her closer—but she was paralyzed in his arms. She tried not to respond, tried to make sense of what was happening.

And then it dawned on Callie like the sky opening above her that Drew was *kissing her.* Flicking the moist tip of his tongue across the sensitive swell at the center of her upper lip, he drew back slightly. She stared into his jewel blue eyes. They were filled with as many questions and yearnings as she felt hers must hold. But he was definitely not teasing. Her head spun in confusion.

"Drew?" she asked softly, as if questioning the identity of the man who held her against him.

One corner of his mouth tipped upward. "Yes, Callie?"

Suddenly, the sensations assaulting her—the texture of Drew's naked chest beneath her palms, his warm hands across her back, the questions in the depths of his eyes— converged and clarified into one, solid impression: *Drew Barnett had kissed her!* And he looked as if he'd like to do it again.

Without thought, Callie smiled joyously and, though still unsure of what he wanted from her, she reacted. She scooted higher on his chest until nose to nose with him, and she kissed him back.

He did tease her then, teased her with a brief bonding of his mouth full against hers before retreating again, smiling as if he too found this moment hard to believe. Then, with a swift movement, Drew placed his thumb on Callie's small cleft chin and opened her to him.

No more teasing, not this time, not this kiss. No—it seared passion along her spine, branding little footsteps racing to her core. Callie kissed him with a fervency produced by years of longing, and she held nothing back. Forget the rationalizing! She loved him, had always loved him. And though she'd acquired enough sense in six years not to blurt out such an admission, Callie couldn't help telling Drew what her heart felt in another way.

"You're so sweet," he murmured, his hands gliding over her, igniting what she had thought already ablaze. "Sweet and natural...like vanilla. Lord, you tempt me, in so many ways. How you fit against me, like you were made to."

He deftly rolled them over, reversing their positions and making Callie wrap her arms around his neck for support. He sank his face into the hollow between collarbone and ear, tasting her warm, soft throat.

She could barely catch her breath. A heaven of possibilities opened above her and Callie began to think that perhaps—oh, just maybe—Drew might have fallen in love with her, too.

He dragged himself away from her throat only to move his lips to hers once more. Their mouths molded to each other, silk on satin, so soft. And Callie sank deeper into the emotions enveloping her. With a thin thread of reason, she wondered, like a child desperate for approval, what she had done at this moment that was so different from other times? What combination of words or actions had besieged him and made him want her now? What new place had she touched?

Her fingers twined in his hair with an urgency born of a thousand dreams. His name drifted on her lips in awe, then became lost within his mouth. She could lose her mind and confuse her own identity, but never would the sharp clarity of how Drew felt against her at this moment blur in her memory.

With a ragged sigh Drew broke the kiss, and Callie felt his arms tremble as he buried his face in her hair. She stroked the back of his head rapturously, her eyes squeezed tightly shut in wonderment. And she found the words she'd promised herself she'd not say springing to her lips as if from a deep, irrepressible fountain.

"Drew. Oh, Drew, I lo—"

"No," he interrupted with a low groan, then more strongly, *"No."*

As quickly as he had come to her, he was gone. Callie lay stunned, her eyes still closed, and the morning air cooled the places on her body that Drew had warmed. She felt as if her very heart had been wrenched from her. *Oh, now what was wrong?*

Slowly, she opened her eyes to a canopy of green and brown. Her gaze sought his figure and found it. He stood a few yards away, arm braced against a tree trunk, the splendidly molded muscles of his naked back tensed, his dark head flung back, housing eyes she couldn't see.

She pushed herself upright as an ominous gnawing began to grow in the pit of her stomach. "Drew?" she asked.

His back expanded as he took a large breath. "I'm sorry, Callie," he said. He turned to face her, and she saw anguish in his eyes. "I shouldn't have kissed you. It was wrong of me—" He broke off, then his next words seemed torn from him.

"But, God, I just wanted . . . so badly. . . When I saw you sitting there, smiling at me so sincerely and so serenely, I felt so *close* to you I had to do something." He set his hands on his hips and turned his gaze upward again, continuing raggedly, "At that moment, I felt I could have convinced you of anything."

"I—I don't understand," Callie said in a strangled voice. Convince her of what? "What did I do? What did you want?" She would give it to him, if only she knew.

"What I want—" Drew shook his head, as if shaking off a persistent fly. His features were drawn and fierce. Distractedly, she realized she'd seen his face look like that another time—when she'd come to his dorm room the night of her graduation.

"What I want shouldn't matter. And it's nothing you did." He closed his eyes and swallowed, his throat working spasmodically. "I care for you, Callie. I'm so very...attracted to you, though I've tried not to be. And I know you're still—" he hesitated over the word, and she felt she would die if he said she was still "sweet" on him. But he finished simply, "—that you care for me, too. But I should never have taken advantage of those feelings. I managed not to six years ago and it would hardly be any more fair for me to do so now."

"What do you mean?" she managed to ask through stricken confusion.

"It's not fair to you, Callie," he stated, as if she would challenge him. "I won't do this to you, not again."

She stared at him, her brain working to make sense of his words. Not fair? To love her, to want her as she did him?

Then it dawned on her. He hadn't mentioned love, not exactly.

A humiliating rash broke out across her cheeks. He *wanted* her. Not loved her. She wasn't so ignorant she failed to recognize the difference between those words. She was strangely relieved to know his attentions toward her weren't for sake of teasing, that she might spark something in him beside platonic affection. But he knew those feelings for what they were, and refrained from ascribing the word "love" to them.

In a world of doubt, Callie began to wonder if what *she* felt was love—six years ago and now. She'd been so sure then, at seventeen. And yet she'd gone on with her life and gotten over him. She'd dated on and off in Los Angeles, and though she knew quite definitely what wasn't love, she fully expected to recognize it when it found her. So now, with Drew, could she be sure? Or did she only wish that what she felt for this man, so close to her heart in so many ways, was love, having no other label that seemed to fit? If she hadn't come back to Iowa, she'd have never had the opportunity to reexplore these feelings and never would have wondered. And she would have been happy. Wouldn't she?

She could not prevent her mind from picturing different scenarios: Perhaps if she'd been older, if the two of them hadn't grown up as neighbors, if she'd come back a few months earlier before he took up with Maura.

Maura. No, it wasn't fair—not if Drew loved Maura.

Callie closed her eyes and choked back profound regret. Yes, she loved Drew Barnett, but the fact remained that time, place, and circumstance had conspired to prevent him from loving her.

Dropping her forehead against her knuckles, Callie stifled a sob of utter desolation. Vaguely, she remembered Drew's long ago admonition, telling her to grow up before playing at love. Well, she'd matured since then, most definitely. Nothing, Callie thought, seasoned a woman like tearing her heart in two.

"Callie?"

She heard his steps as he drew near, and she made herself raise her head and meet his concerned eyes.

"I should never have come back," she said dully. She couldn't take this torment.

"Ah, Callie." The words were a groan. "Ah, Callie, this is what I hoped would never happen." He stood only a few feet in front of her as she knelt on the soft ground. "I'm so terribly sorry I've held any part in making you feel that way. You've been clear about how you feel and what's important to you. I just haven't abided by it."

At his words, she lost the battle of maintaining eye contact and dropped her gaze. "Then, please," she whispered with the last vestige of her pride, "leave me alone, Drew. I don't want your help. I just want you to leave me alone."

Drew said nothing, and Callie continued to stare at his boots. Then she felt his open hand on the top of her head, a firm pressure, almost in consolation. She swallowed convulsively.

"All right, Callie. I'll leave you alone."

He moved away, stooped, picked up his shirt and shrugged into it. Then he knelt and started gathering cooking utensils together. "Why don't you go call Hannah and we'll get this place cleaned up and go home," he suggested quietly.

Callie rose onto numb legs, watching him, and already she felt her heart begin to grieve the loss of a morning that had started so beautifully. The loss of a friendship that perhaps had never had a chance. "What about catching your catfish?" she asked over the lump in her throat.

Drew looked up at her, his eyes revealing his own regret. "Don't worry. This creek's not going anywhere. I have a whole lifetime to come back and fish this spot." He straightened and kicked dirt over the coals still smoldering in a pile. "A whole lifetime."

Chapter Ten

Callie tramped through the damp, knee-high grass, heading toward the creek, Hannah in the lead and carving a meandering path of her own. May had definitely come to Iowa, painting the morning skies a watercolor shade of cornflower blue under oyster-hued clouds. The clean, sweet scent of wild clover filled the air, and everywhere was nature's industry.

She'd gotten in the habit of walking down this way, always toward the creek, then a half mile along its banks in one direction or another. Hannah and she would start off each morning when the dew was still thick, before Hank pulled up to share a day of hard work on the house. Drew no longer joined them.

Callie drew a lungful of breath. Just a week to go now, she shifted her thoughts with effort, before the open house, timed to coincide with the Memorial Day weekend. A week from today and she'd be gone. Gone for good, she thought painfully.

She swallowed past the tightening in her throat and raised her chin, making herself smile. For now, at least, she was still in Iowa, and the early mornings, just after breakfast, those were still for her and Hannah. And her reflections.

Despite her resistance, Drew was the main occupant of her thoughts nowadays. She hadn't had a private word with him in almost three weeks. The B&B subcommittee met regularly, and though the atmosphere wasn't quite so easy-going, still the two of them managed to function around Hank and Maura. Callie and Drew had become polite strangers, and she wondered how long it would be this way. Each time the answer sounded clearly, as clearly as the rooster's crow carried to her on the spring breeze with vibrant clarity. *Always*.

Callie reached down and plucked a milkweed pod from its stem. She broke the pod open and enjoyed the waft of silky, white fluff as it scattered in an updraft. She wished life were always like this: a beautiful day waiting to be enjoyed, a purpose one was happy to fulfill. On a day like today, she knew with a certainty she could return to Iowa to live. But could she, though, with Drew so near?

No, it wasn't possible.

So she'd return to Los Angeles. And do so happily, for truly, she loved her work. Renovating her parents' home had only reemphasized the point. Because of that experience, she'd be able to reaffirm her purpose back in California. And maybe there she'd put Drew Barnett from her mind for good.

She reached into her jeans' pocket, feeling for the small, smooth orb that had become a talisman. She fished the buckeye out with two fingers. Her lucky buckeye. *Everybody needs one,* Drew had said. She rubbed her thumb over the chestnut eye and it swam before her. In the months to come, she certainly would need some luck.

Hannah had reached the creek before Callie, and the spaniel sat panting happily, her black, glossy fur slick with dew, her muzzle dripping.

She's looking trimmer these days, Callie thought, with the diet and additional exercise. It was going to be hard to leave

Hannah when the time came. *So hard to leave everyone.* Again, her eyes filled, and she blinked rapidly.

"Well, Hannah, which way today?" Callie sank onto a log, breathing deeply of the damp air. She glanced over at Hannah, who was barely containing her impatience. "Okay," Callie relented. "You choose the trail today. I'll follow along in a minute."

She watched the spaniel trot off. No, she wouldn't mind coming back to this sort of life. Even with all the glamour and glitter, L.A. paled in comparison to Iowa's vibrant colors. There was a through-and-through quality to life here— not a veneer or a coat of gloss. Digging deeply, one continued to find what had appeared on the surface—and that included the people of Iowa.

Drew was one of those people. Not a complicated man, but one who didn't shy away from life's trials or obstacles. He possessed a courage, such a capacity for selfless love that she admired and which had drawn her to him years ago.

Callie sighed. *Drew again.* She rose to follow Hannah. Ten minutes later she wished she'd been less free with her consent, as she plowed through waist-high bracken in the spaniel's wake.

"Hannah!" she called, stopping to put her hands on her hips. "I didn't mean for you to take the Overland Pass!" She heard a familiar bark a few yards ahead and plunged on. "Hannah!"

Hannah's excited barking led her to a small clearing not far away, and as she broke into it Callie gasped when she saw what had excited the dog.

Hannah was crouched in a playful position with her behind wagging furiously. At Callie's approach, she had turned her head and given a proud, happy "woof." It wasn't every day that she scared up a black-and-white striped kitty.

"Hannah," Callie said in a low voice, backing away slowly, "that's not a playmate. Come on, girl, let's just leave the nice kitty alone—"

The skunk turned, and Callie would have avoided the thick spray that diffused into an oily mist had she not

tripped in her haste to get away. She came down on her behind, her raised arms and hands ineffectually blocking the
tail end of the drizzle. Hannah, receiving the full force,
backed up in a speedy reverse. She bumped into Callie, who
was sprawled on the ground, and then quickly sat down beside her. Both of them blinked and watched the skunk tod-
dle off into the bushes.

"Oh, Hannah! Oh, *yuck!*" Callie held her arms out from
her sides and glanced around, wondering what she could
wipe her face on. Hannah shook her head and sneezed,
dousing Callie in yet another shower. "Thanks, girl," she
said sarcastically, reaching for the tail of her long-sleeved
shirt. "You're a princess."

The odor was overpowering. She stood, thereby avoiding
another of Hannah's sneezes. Good grief, what was she going to do now? She had never come across a skunk in the
wild, although she remembered one of their other dogs getting a dose of skunk one time before. Her father had taken
the dog out by the barn and drenched him in tomato juice
before scrubbing him with detergent. She dismally realized
that whatever provisions Nate had long ago stocked her
cupboards with, a couple of gallons of tomato juice was not
among them.

Callie glanced around, trying to figure out just where the
two of them were, and concluded that they actually weren't
far from the Barnett homestead. She bit her lower lip, hes-
itating a moment. She could always go back to the house, to
wait or make a phone call. But Hank wouldn't arrive for
more than an hour, and there was no way Callie intended to
enter her house in this condition. Even if she touched nothing, the smell would linger for weeks.

She really had no choice.

She glanced down at Hannah, who caught the look in
Callie's eye. The spaniel lowered her head in shame, flat-
tened her body to the ground and tried to skulk away, as if
Callie wouldn't notice a black-haired, fifty-five-pound
moving rock.

"Oh, no you don't." Callie grabbed the dog's thick collar. "We're in this together, mutt."

Drew was just coming out of the barn when he spotted Callie climbing over the back fence and Hannah squeezing under it. He watched them walk toward him, his puzzlement obvious at Callie's reddened complexion and Hannah's uncharacteristically docile gait.

"Hello, Callie," he said unsmilingly. "You're up early, aren't—" He stopped and grimaced as they came into sniffing range. "Phew! What the hell did you get into?"

She pointed an accusing finger at Hannah. "*Hannah* got into a tussle with a pretty wood-kitty." She glanced at Drew. "We were walking along the creek when she scared up a skunk. Neither of us could get out of the way in time."

Drew was instantly at her side, despite the strength of the pungent scent that cloaked her, her hands in his as he examined them and her arms. "A skunk? You didn't get bit, did you?"

"No, no," she assured him. "Just a shower. Hannah got a full dose. I just got the fallout." She shook her hands helplessly after he dropped them, her eyes watering at the pervading odor. "Please, Drew, help us."

Hannah, obviously sensing an ally in her good buddy Drew, sidled toward him. He backed away hurriedly, waving a hand in front of his face. "Wait a minute. Let me get upwind of you two. Lord, what a smell! Don't you know enough to run when you see a skunk?"

"Of course I do!" Callie protested indignantly, hands on her hips. "I just—well, I tripped and fell down, and the next thing I knew—" She started laughing in spite of herself. It was so ridiculous. And Drew looked so thoroughly disgusted with the both of them.

She sobered. "All right, it was a clumsy move. Aren't you going to help us anyway?"

"I'm thinking about it." He rubbed his hand over his chin. "Look, you two just sit tight for a minute while I run into town and get some tomato juice." He started for the

Bronco, turning back as a thought struck him. "And for God's sake, don't touch anything! I don't need my whole place stinking to high heaven." He started the truck and drove off.

When he returned half an hour later, he found Callie and Hannah sitting disconsolately on a sufficiently isolated old stump in the yard. He carried two cases of tomato juice and set one on the back step before taking the other into the house. A minute later he returned with several old towels. He tossed Callie one of them as she abandoned the stump and trudged over to him.

"Here," he said, "take off your clothes and wrap this around you."

"Take off my clothes?" she exclaimed fractiously, gesturing at the great outdoors all around them. The skunk odor had given her a headache, and her mood had deteriorated from bad to worse. "Here? I will not!"

"Then plan on taking your tomato juice rinse outside with Hannah, because I'm not letting you tramp through my house in those things to use my bathroom and get it any more smelly than it has to be."

"But I'm not going to strip out here in broad daylight!"

He glanced around. "There's nobody to see."

"There's you," she protested.

Drew rolled his eyes and said dryly, "I've seen most of it before. But I'll turn around." He obliged by doing so.

Callie had no choice but to try to keep the towel covering the important areas while she wriggled out of her jeans and shirt. "When?"

"When what?" Drew asked.

"When have you seen most of... it?"

"Oh. Jeez, I don't know." She could see him uncross his arms and scratch his left cheek with his right hand. "When you used to run through the sprinkler in nothing but your training pants? When you—"

"Fine!" Callie wrapped the towel around her and tucked an end securely between her breasts. There really was an inordinate amount of history between them that did not lend itself to romantic liaisons.

"Done?" Drew asked and turned to discover she was. "Good. Now put everything in this plastic bag. Anything in here you can't live without?"

"Why?" Callie asked, complying.

"I'm going to have to burn these clothes. They're hopeless."

"Burn them!" She dug into the bag. "But those are my favorite sneakers." She produced them and stared up at him imploringly. "They didn't get sprayed. Can't I keep them?"

He took them from her and, holding them at arm's length, sniffed none too heartily. "It's hard to tell what stinks around here and what doesn't." He set the sneakers down on the step. "Let them air for a while and we'll see. Come on, Hannah."

His eyes briefly went over Callie's skimpy attire before he turned and started toward the barn, a case of tomato juice on his shoulder and Hannah trailing along behind him. "I put the other case of juice upstairs in the bathroom with a can opener," he called over his shoulder. "Rinse yourself off good, especially your hair. Then wash it a couple of times with the shampoo I set out. I'm going to take care of Hannah."

Nearly an hour later Callie had done just that, and in water up to her shoulders she sat soaking the last of the skunk from her pores. Her headache had disappeared and she was trying to ignore the cooling of the water.

She soaped her washcloth again and trailed it up her arm and over her shoulder. She wished the bathroom at her parents' had a tub like this: a big, old thing set up high on claw feet. Drew must have replaced the fixtures on it, for they were a shiny, new brass. In fact, he must have done a lot of work on the bathroom. She noticed the same bright fixtures on the old-fashioned sink, and the wainscoting and eggshell-white paint on the walls looked new. Porcelain towel rods held thick, dark green towels, and an oval rug of the same deep green lay on the dark wood floor.

With regret, she finally pulled the plug and rose to dry herself. She'd stepped out of the tub and was blotting her feet when she thought about clothes. Or the lack of them, actually.

She had nothing to wear and nowhere to get it.

Callie stared into a small, wood-framed mirror frosted around the edges with steam. Her large violet eyes, surrounded by wet, spiky lashes, filled with apprehension. How did she manage to get into these predicaments? She felt suddenly like the main character in some inane sitcom whose sole entertainment value centered on the juvenile lead's difficult straits. She recalled Drew's manner at seeing her: a little disgusted, inconvenienced. Yes, he'd admitted he was attracted to her, but obviously times like this reinforced his forbearance.

Callie pushed her damp, tangled hair from her face and wrapped the large towel around her. She needed to get out of there, out of Drew's life once and for all.

Cautiously, she opened and peeked out the bathroom door. No sounds rose from downstairs. She spied an open door of what looked like a bedroom. Tiptoeing, she made her way down the hallway, cringing at every squeak in the floorboards. Once there, she wasted little time looking around as she opened the drawer of a large highboy and began pawing stealthily through its contents.

"Can I help you?"

Callie spun, her fingers clamped in a death grip on the terry knot at her breast. Drew stood in the open doorway.

He sniffed experimentally. "Well, I have to admit it smells better up here than I expected." He moved to the window and cracked it open, apparently oblivious to her strangled gasp as Callie backed against the open drawer.

"I was looking for a shirt or some shorts or something," she explained lamely. "To wear."

"Let me see what I can find." He crossed to the highboy, his arm brushing her shoulder as he reached around her. Callie felt paralyzed, fearful that any movement would compound the awkwardness of her situation. Drew took out a neatly folded plaid shirt. He glanced down at Callie questioningly and she stared back, rooted. Finally, he reached his other arm around her, closed the open drawer and opened the one below it, nudging her in the behind. His eyes remained locked with hers, until he looked into the drawer and pulled out a pair of boxer shorts.

He held up shorts and shirt. "Will these do?"

Callie felt her cheeks flame as her eyes took in the surprisingly bright-colored pattern on the boxer shorts. "Y-yes." She took them from him, regaining some of her composure. "I'll be the height of fashion."

He raised a brow quizzically.

"Boxer shorts are all the rage for the casually dressed L.A. coed."

"Just boxer shorts?"

"And T-shirts. The ribbed, tank-style kind."

For the first time, Drew smiled. "I'm beginning to think California *does* have its attractions," he murmured.

She felt her face grow even hotter and muffled a sigh of relief as Drew moved away. He leaned on the bolster of a large rice bed that she hadn't previously noticed. She glanced quickly away.

"Hannah's cleaned up," he informed her, "although she's going to smell a little like eau de Pepe LePew for a few days." He crossed his arms thoughtfully. "She must have stumbled across a mother skunk with a litter. Skunks are nocturnal and usually very docile. They rarely spray unless provoked or rabid. That's why I was concerned that you hadn't been bitten. Hannah's had her rabies shot, but I don't think you've been inoculated."

"Not lately," she said crisply. A slight draft through the window gave her goose bumps that rose in numerous places across her body. She had scant protection against either the breeze or Drew's penetrating gaze.

She moved away from the draft to a waist-high dresser on the adjoining wall. Leaning against the edge of it, she chafed the bottom of one foot over the top of the other as Drew continued to lounge against the bedpost.

"Are you going to stand there all day?" she finally asked.

His eyes, which had seemed merely interested before, became a wicked blue. He appeared to give the matter a moment of thought.

"Are you?" he asked.

"Of course not!" She caught the gleam in his eye. "*You're* the skunk around here, Drew Barnett. Why don't you leave, so I can get dressed and get out of your hair?"

"I had to see how my guest was doing," he replied solicitously.

"Your guest?"

"I've been thinking I might get into the inn business myself, you've made it sound so profitable." He clasped one hand over the other in front of him and regarded her earnestly. "A good innkeeper would hardly let his guest run out of towels or soap or something."

"Well. As you can see, I have plenty of towels, and I'm done with the soap, thank you, so you're discharged of your duties." She managed to sound confident, but her insides trembled. What was he up to?

"I do see. But I doubt the truly conscientious innkeeper would be so easily appeased." Drew pushed off from the bolster and sauntered over, until he stood directly in front of her. With the dresser already against the back of her legs, Callie had no escape as he moved closer still. With one hand she clutched the clothes to her chest, the other fumbling behind her for balance.

"You're not an innkeeper, Drew," she said breathlessly. Was he teasing her, yet again? How could he torment her so?

"You could teach me, though, couldn't you?" was his cryptic question, his face mere inches from hers. He lifted his hand and the tips of his fingers grazed her cheek. "I want to learn, Callie. I promise I'll do whatever it takes..."

His hand slid under her chin and her knees nearly buckled as she closed her eyes, remembering when he had touched her this way last. No, he wasn't teasing, but he couldn't mean it either.

"Stop!" Callie cried, unable to take any more. "I can't stand it, Drew. Please. I can't let you do this to me." She opened her eyes and stared at him, not caring if everything she felt for him showed in her eyes—she simply had to get him away from her!

It worked. He stepped back and shook his head, as if coming to his senses. They stood for a moment, staring at each other.

Finally Drew sighed and looked away. "You're right, Callie," he said quietly. "I shouldn't have come in here." He turned away from her, as if seeking to conceal his expression from her. "Hannah will be with me in the barn when you're finished dressing. Your shoes are still on the back step." He half turned, digging into his pocket. He held a small object out to her. "I found something I thought you might want."

Into her hand dropped the buckeye, warm and glossy.

Callie closed her fingers around it. Her gaze flew to his face, searching for...what? But he thwarted her by turning away again. She heard his retreating tread as he left her alone.

She unwrapped the towel and hurried to shrug into the large shirt, resisting the urge to close her eyes and bury her face in the fabric. To distract herself, she glanced around as she buttoned the shirt. Here was where the walnut armoire would have gone, she realized instantly, and she could see why Drew might have wanted it. It would have complemented perfectly the room's pale walls, accented by the dark wood moldings. The high bed was covered with a patchwork quilt in reds and greens. Along with the dresser and highboy, a plaid-covered stuffed chair sat in a corner, completing the furniture in the room. Her designer's eye missed nothing.

An inn, she thought as she donned the boxer shorts, again banishing the wayward images that assaulted her as the elastic slid over her hips. Drew must have spent some time redoing this room and the bathroom, and the effect was pleasing. She pictured him here, working with loving hands, much as she did, to make this house once again his home.

Oh, Drew, Drew. As he worked in this room, perhaps stopping now and then, leaning back on his heels and running a forearm across his brow as he surveyed his progress, she wondered if he had thought of Maura, of bringing her here. Of offering this house and himself as proof of his love. Needing nothing else.

Callie faced herself in the mirror above the dresser. It was time. Time to forgive and be forgiven, and go on. She wouldn't leave Iowa with even a trace of enmity between her and Drew. She had to do that much, even if, as before, she left because of him.

Five minutes later she found Drew where he had said he'd be, currying a huge roan stallion that was obviously Sancho. She stood just inside the door for a moment, admiring his long, sure strokes and loving the way he talked softly to the large beast, his voice at a pitch that hovered between murmur and whisper. He turned when she approached. Hannah, also clean and damp, padded up to her, sniffing her hand for pardon.

"He's beautiful, Drew," she said, keeping her step toward the man and his horse as soft as her voice. The stallion reared his head anyway, his eye wild as it gazed down on her.

"Shh. Come on, fella," Drew coaxed. "It's just Callie. She won't hurt you, you big lug."

She paused outside the horse's stall and stepped up on the rail, quietly watching the superb male animal. She put out a tentative hand. "Hey, boy," she crooned.

Sancho turned his head and for a measuring minute looked at her, black eyes gleaming. Then he snuffled her hand, begging her touch.

Drew raised his eyebrow. "Well, well. He's usually tough to get to know."

"I don't have a problem getting to know animals most of the time." Too late, she recalled his words, nearly the same.

She scratched the glossy chestnut neck that was offered to her, once again unable to meet Drew's eyes.

Drew moved to the stallion's other side, now facing her as he brushed the horse. He whisked the sturdy comb across Sancho's finely molded withers as she watched, mesmerized. "Why haven't you turned him out?"

"I usually do, but the farrier's coming to shoe him later today. Jesse would never forgive me for making him shoe a stallion who had to be caught and was feeling his oats."

Callie stroked the stallion's strong, broad nose. "I can see why Pavlova succumbed so easily," she said lightly.

"Yeah, Pavlova didn't have a chance, did she, Sancho?" Drew grunted as he applied the large comb to the horse's black mane. "She was a real pushover. I brought her here, the two of them took one look at each other and that was it."

Callie glanced around. "Here? This is where it took place?"

"No, no room in here. I turned them loose in the south pasture." Drew hung the currycomb on a hook and gave Sancho a last pat as he left the stall, latching it on his way out.

"Oh," she breathed as he came to stand beside her.

He rested his forearms on the rail next to her. "It was beautiful, two great animals, coming together like that. There's something fierce and frightening in it," he said softly, "but what struck me was its inevitability. They both capitulated to it, they both realized they had no choice."

He glanced at her. "Sorry. I forget this isn't one of your favorite topics."

"No need to be sorry," she murmured, concentrating her gaze on her fingernail as it picked at a splinter on the wooden rail. "Drew—" she began, just as he said . . . "Callie—"

Both stopped. "Go ahead," he obliged.

"I only wanted to say—" She gave off fooling with the splinter and grasped the top of the rail with both hands.

"I'm sorry for what happened that day by the creek. I mean, I'm sorry it was so...unpleasant."

"It was my fault, Callie."

"Yes, it was," she admitted softly. "It was both our faults, for not understanding each other. Or ourselves." She finally looked up at him. "This time when I leave I don't want to go away hurt and angry for either of us not being what the other wants." She smiled crookedly. "You know, you've always been my hero, Drew. As much as Nate, you've been my big brother—picking me up out of the dirt when I fell and scraped my knees, defending me from bullies. Enduring my trailing along..."

She closed her eyes briefly. "Anyway, I didn't want to go away without saying..."

She'd almost slipped up. *It doesn't make a difference. He loves Maura.* "Thank you, Drew," she finished simply.

He searched her face intently. Then he pushed away and turned. "Come on. I'll give you a lift home." He walked across the barn, away from her.

Callie stared after him a moment, then she took a step. "Drew, wait."

He stopped but didn't turn around.

"Drew—" *Don't do it,* she thought desperately. *Don't make that mistake, not again.* Clearly, he had no desire to listen to any more of her outpourings. He was finished dealing with her and perhaps wanted more than she for her to avoid embarrassing herself again. She wished she hadn't started the conversation.

But she had to say it. Like Sancho and Pavlova, she did not have a choice in saying it. Because she knew, as surely as her own heart beat within her chest, that she loved Drew Barnett. And if she failed to tell him so, she'd leave feeling less resolved with what she felt for him than when she had left six years ago. He had to hear it, not from the mouth of a willful seventeen-year-old, but from the mouth of a grown woman who knew her mind and heart.

"You'll always be the first man I ever loved, Drew," she said. Ah, almost, but not quite: *I love you.*

"Callie—" His head fell back. "Don't. Don't do this to me, or to yourself. I told you—you were right. You were right to leave years ago, right to leave again." He started walking away from her again.

Callie stared after him as stunned seconds ticked past. Then her furious voice arrested his retreat. "Drew Barnett, stop right there!"

He turned and she marched up to him. "Don't you *dare* make it sound like it was my idea to leave here six years ago! My God, Drew, you told me to go!"

"I had to," he insisted, glaring down at her. "I had no right, no good reason to ask you to stay."

She clamped her teeth over a denial to his assumption. *Don't argue with him,* she told herself. *It won't change a thing.*

"So fine, we both did what we thought we had to. Now let's just let it pass." Her eyes searched his face. "That's all I want. Truly, there's nothing else. Can't we do that?"

He swallowed hard. "You're leaving Iowa again."

"That has nothing to do with it, Drew!"

His hands shot out and closed over her upper arms. "Nothing to *do* with it?" he asked, incredulous. "You've made it pretty damned clear it has everything to do with it and it still isn't enough!"

"*What* isn't enough?" she asked, thoroughly confused.

"This!" And his mouth descended to hers.

Callie's head fell back as he crushed her against him, his grasp tightening on her upper arms. Her senses reeled with the closeness of him, the vibrancy of him. His lips dragged against hers as he moved them in a forceful rotation. She fisted her hands, bringing her bent arms up and outward, struggling against his grip. He released her suddenly, as if he realized how harshly he held her. But Callie only wrapped her arms around his neck and pulled him closer still, wanting, in spite of the damage it might do her, this last moment in his arms. Drew responded with a groan, hooking his thumbs under her arms and digging his fingers into her shoulder blades.

He lifted his head, blue eyes blazing, her own frustration mirrored in his scowl. "I swear I don't understand you," he muttered huskily.

"That makes two of us," Callie acknowledged. They both breathed heavily, bringing their chests into contact, then apart, then together again. With a low groan, Drew pulled her into his arms, pressing her head against his chest as his chin rested on her hair.

"Callie, Callie. What's going on here?" He drew away slightly, gazing down into her face. The corner of his mouth lifted. "You mean you don't understand you, or you don't understand me?"

"Yes."

The moment held, suspended. Only the sounds of Hannah going round and round in a circle, searching for a comfortable spot in the hay, and Sancho's intermittent pawing disturbed the powerful silence. Callie felt the strength of emotion that hung in the air between them.

Emotion—as in passion, not love, she thought. And Drew was right. It still wasn't enough. He was attracted to her. *Wanted* her. He'd never once mentioned love, though she had, more than once. He knew what she wanted from him, and she would settle for nothing less.

I want what he feels for Maura.

Thinking of the woman the two of them now betrayed, Callie broke her hold around Drew's neck and let her arms slide down his chest. A hot blanket of shame swept over her. How could she do this to Maura? And how could Drew?

She pushed out of his arms and turned away, mortified.

"Callie, what's wrong?" his puzzled voice came from behind her.

"I can't believe I acted this way," she said into her hands.

"What way?"

"How could we? Oh, Maura—"

"Maura?" Drew's hand on her shoulder turned her toward him. "What's Maura got to do with this?"

She stared up at him, horrified he could be so unfeeling, wondering if she was so ignorant of the relationships between men and women that his reaction would seem so distorted. "Drew, you can't mean—"

"You thought," he interrupted as comprehension dawned on his face. "You think there's something between Maura and me?"

Callie blinked. "Is—isn't there?"

He shook his head slowly, assessing her. "Maura's a friend, yes, but nothing more. And she . . . I don't think she does, but if she feels something more for me, I've never had any indication of it."

"Oh." Callie pressed her palms to her flushed cheeks, her gaze shifting sightlessly as she tried to sort her whirling thoughts.

Drew doesn't love Maura. The realization shot through her, but not in exhilaration. Her error only compounded her confusion, and she wondered what else she'd misinterpreted. What if Drew *did* love her, Callie? The things he'd said—it was possible. But if so, what was wrong? He constantly resisted her—because she was his "adopted" little sister and could never be anything more? Because she had no knowledge of how a man *wants* or needs or loves?

Or why?

She found Drew's eyes on her, watching her reaction. "Does that change the situation between us, Callie?" he asked softly.

"I don't know. Does it?"

He compressed his lips and took a deep breath. "I don't know, either. You're still going back to California. You've got to." Drew studied her. "I can't do it to you again. Don't you see that?"

"See what?"

"You have so much to give, Callie. So many dreams to fulfill. You promised me you wouldn't give them up and I won't let you do it, even now when I can see that I could." He looked at her bleakly. "I was the reason you left Iowa. I won't be the reason now you abandon your dreams."

She stared at him. No, she didn't see. It sounded as if he *did* care for her, but if so it wasn't enough, just as he'd said.

With effort, she tried to sort it out: He didn't love Maura and he knew Callie loved him; he cared for her, but she was going back to California. He wanted her to go....

Callie shook her head as if that would put her thoughts into place. It didn't help. He didn't love her, couldn't love her if he still wanted her to go.

"I've got to get out of here," Callie said numbly, not sure if she meant her immediate surroundings or the entire state of Iowa.

Drew took a step toward her. "I think that's a good idea. I'll give you a ride," he said, obviously taking the former meaning.

She stepped away from him. "No. I'll walk home."

He put out a hand to stop her, but she'd swept past him.

And she didn't walk home. She ran the entire way, Hannah chasing after her.

Chapter Eleven

Memorial Day dawned warm and humid. The people of Soldier Creek, Iowa were pleased, though. At least it wasn't raining. An approaching low-pressure front meant a storm by tomorrow, but that was then. This was now, and the sun was a welcome participant in the simple program.

Callie and Nate stood toward the back of the crowd that had assembled to watch the ceremonies, replete with nostalgic impressions. The ladies' groups had decorated the makeshift podium in red, white and blue, and its homespun quality contributed to other unintentional vignettes of small-town life. The local Boy Scout troop was first down a lane bordered by flower-ladened headstones, marching in an imprecise but earnest step. A few cubs clutched with unScout-like timidity the hands of their den mothers. Then the local American Legion, carrying national, state and legion flags, approached the small assembly waiting at the edge of the cemetery, near the white crosses marked with red poppies. After a brief benediction, the crowd heard speeches by Otie Slater and the district's current state representative, both of whom were unable to resist the opportunity to address their constituencies.

The talent was all homegrown but well received. A local girl in a flowered dress that looked as if it might have been worn to a relative's wedding several years earlier, sang the national anthem in an insubstantial voice, never quite making the high notes. To conclude the program, a high-school trumpet player performed taps, and another trumpet at the far side of the cemetery echoed the haunting tune in wavering tones, in this instance entirely appropriate. Members of the American Legion, ex-serviceman all, closed the observances with a three-gun salute.

Afterward, Callie caught sight of Maura as she placed a bouquet on Wayne Foster's grave. Across the rows of headstones, she watched as Drew, so tall beside his mother, did the same by his father's grave. They stopped to chat with Maura, and Callie felt an odd twinge. She realized now that Drew's attention to Maura was the same as the concern he'd shown Callie and Nate—the ingrained caring, that special brand of midwestern gentility that had raised barns a century ago and continued in the people of Iowa today.

Callie and Nate drove back to the inn and Maura joined them in time to help Callie uncover trays of cookies and put an ice ring into the punch bowl of lemonade. Before long, they were entertaining a steady stream of the curious.

Callie's heart nearly burst with pride as she watched car after car pull onto the driveway now laid with new pea gravel. Hank had painted the shutters and trim a dark green, and flowers rimmed the house in a border of color. Just yesterday she had suspended a wooden sign from hooks that hung above the new mailbox: *Farrell Guest House—A Country Inn.*

Each room had taken on a personality that said, "Come, enjoy my comforts." The sitting room conveyed coziness and welcome, with books arranged in casual disarray. Sally Farrell's prized willowware vase overflowed with large pink-and-white peonies on the antique coffee table. A ceiling fan stirred the ponderous air and the lace curtains at the windows. Hannah's nails click-clicked across the refinished wood floors as she rose from her post by the fireplace to greet each new visitor.

Upstairs, the bedrooms formed a glad mixture of impressions. Brightly colored locally made quilts covered the large, high beds and were enhanced by embroidered pillow shams. Hank had done a beautiful job on the tiny half baths in each of the rooms, and Maura had placed the antique tea set out on a side table in one room, as if to say that everything was ready and waiting for the next guest.

They had visitors from as far away as Des Moines, all of whom delighted in the bit of Americana Callie had constructed. Many of the callers exclaimed over the inventive, economical ways Callie had found to establish the inn's rustic ambience, and as she was deluged with questions she realized her efforts would impact these people long after she'd left. The new lake was a shot in the arm to the area, the beginning of a slightly different way of life that would allow the old way to continue. And even though it would be Maura who would complete the organization and setting up of the referral network, Callie was proud she'd helped, in her own way, in preserving the town's heritage.

The only tense moment of the afternoon came when Drew appeared with his mother. "I've been dying of curiosity ever since you and Nate decided to start this inn," said Alice Barnett, her hair now more gray than black. Callie's chest became ever tighter as she escorted Alice and her son on a personal tour of the inn, and as they walked through the rooms Callie had worked on with Drew she felt again that burden of regret that she would no longer share such moments with him. But Alice unwittingly alleviated some of the strain with her lively questions and comments. She seemed extremely interested in the inn and Callie got her to promise to supply Maura with some of her elderberry jam—with fair compensation, of course.

Just as Drew and his mother were leaving, Cora Lawsen descended the stairs, having completed her own guided tour, courtesy of Hank. They gathered near the front door.

"Well, Callie." Cora fastened her astute scrutiny on the younger woman. "You've done a fine job. You and Nate. I know your parents are proud of you."

Callie met Drew's impenetrable gaze across his mother's gray head. "Thank you, Cora. But we couldn't have done it alone. Not without Hank and Maura and Drew."

Cora nodded. "Just so, just so. I understand the referral network is coming along?"

"Maura is taking my place as chairperson of the committee, and Nate has agreed to serve on the committee until Mother comes back."

Again, a satisfied nod from Cora. "So you're leaving again?"

"Yes. Tomorrow afternoon."

Cora went on matter-of-factly, "Well, I daresay you'll come back to visit a little more often, with the inn and everything. You've put so much effort into it, I can't imagine you'll be able to stay away."

"Perhaps," Callie answered with a strained smile. Cora really pushed the limits of her authority. "I'm leaving the inn in good hands with Maura. And Mom and Dad will be back before long. I doubt I'll be needed."

"Fresh faces like yours are always needed around here." She surprised Callie with a brief kiss on the cheek. "Goodbye, dear. Come along, Henry."

Callie and Hank shared a grin behind Cora's already departing back. Despite the appearance of being led around, Hank seemed no worse for wear. Callie knew he was in good hands.

He gave her a hug. "Mercy, girl, I'll miss you."

Then it was Drew's turn to say his goodbyes. "The inn's a credit to you, Callie," he said quietly. "You've done what you set out to do."

Have I? she wanted to ask. Her purpose in returning to Iowa had indeed been accomplished. Only time would tell if her purpose in leaving it would bear similar results.

"Thank you for your help in getting me there, Drew," she said. She recalled the moments they'd shared, the closeness that she would never relinquish—not even with the pain she felt now. "Thank you for being my friend."

"I wish I could have done more," he said in an echo of her words as they'd stood outside his clinic while inside a boy grieved for his dog. She met his eyes briefly, but glanced away as she felt her heart sink with a grief all its own. *Please,* it begged, *I can't take any more.*

"Goodbye, Drew."

She turned away rather than watch him leave, but she heard every footstep echoing hollowly on the porch, every crunch across the gravel, the slam of first one car door, then the other.

And then he was gone. But the pain remained.

The wind picked up by the time Maura and Callie ushered the last of the visitors out the door. They stood on the porch waving goodbye and enjoying the breeze after the heat of the day. Nate came banging out the screen door and stood behind them.

"I'd better be getting back to my place and get the stock situated before this storm blows in," he said. "Can I give you a lift home, Maura?"

Maura brushed a strand of golden hair out of her eyes, glancing over her shoulder at Nate. As Callie watched, a blush spread over Maura's delicate skin and her lashes fluttered downward. "Thanks, Nate, I have my own car."

Callie's brows rose in speculation as her gaze shifted to observe her brother's reaction. His eyes rested musingly on Maura's face.

Callie recalled the conversation she'd had with him, that morning when she'd first returned home. Clearly, she pictured his rueful smile as he told her not to pine over Drew. *He and Maura Foster have been going around together ever since he came back to Soldier Creek. Everyone's expecting a wedding by fall.*

Perhaps Nate did dream of something else, something more besides farming.

She'd always wondered why Nate had never said any-thing more about the matter, as good a friend as he was to Drew. Maybe Nate hadn't wanted to dwell on a romance between Maura and his best friend any more than Callie had, though for different reasons.

She wondered idly, knowing now that there was nothing between Maura and Drew, how the last two months might have been different—had she known from the beginning that the two were not romantically involved. She couldn't imagine the outcome would have changed that much. Drew knew she loved him, and still it was not enough. Though he cared for her, that wasn't enough, not for what she needed from him. At least he'd been honest about it, six years ago and now.

Nate nodded briefly at Maura's refusal. "Guess I'll be shoving off, then."

The two women bade him goodbye, then entered the house. They returned leftover cookies to their storage containers and wiped down the dining-room table and kitchen counters.

"Well," Maura said when they had finished, her hands on her hips, "I think we could call today an unqualified success."

"Oh, certainly. Daisy Curtis from the *Sycamore County Times* said she'd write a review in exchange for a free night's lodging. That'll save you some of the advertising budget and probably do more good than an ad would have done. And once we get more inns participating in the network, she'll be an excellent source."

"I'll call her next week to schedule her," Maura answered. "Can you believe we're already booked halfway through June?"

Callie brushed an imaginary speck of dust from the top of the toaster. "I wish we had more bookings." Seeing Maura's expression, she said, "But don't worry. It'll pick up through the summer."

"I hope so." Maura said, forehead still creased. Callie had to laugh at her. Maura was so earnest, as if this inn were her own family's undertaking.

"Maura, Maura," she chided gently, "it'll all work out. What could go wrong?"

"The parks-and-recreation department could find man-eating alligators in the lake?"

"Then we'd start making alligator boots," Callie said with a straight face.

"I can sew some mean decorative stitching," Maura deadpanned back. They laughed at their whimsy.

"Oh, Callie," Maura said, ending a laugh. "I wish you didn't have to leave, even though it would put me out of a job."

"You know something, Maura?" Callie leaned her elbows on the counter and gazed out the kitchen window. "I don't want to leave. But somehow I don't see myself staying, either."

Maura stood behind her as Callie studied the red-topped farmhouse in the distance. Callie felt the other woman's touch on her shoulder, brief but comforting. "You know, don't you, that if you should decide to stay and run the inn and referral network yourself, that you're not to worry about me. Although running the inn would be lovely, Davey and I are doing just fine."

"Thank you, Maura." Callie smiled and straightened resolutely. "But I'm not even thinking of staying."

Maura nodded. "See you in the morning then."

Callie herded the chickens into their coop before walking to the barn to check on Pavlova. The mare seemed fine, although she shied a little from Callie's touch. Callie filled her feed trough with oats and replenished her water.

"I guess you're not a real fan of thunderstorms either, huh, Pav?" she asked the skittish horse in her most soothing tones. "Well, you'll be nice and dry in here." She took a few moments to pet and talk to the mare, knowing that her time was near.

Pavlova calmed under her mistress's gentle ministrations. Callie's eyes followed her hands as they ran comforting paths down the smooth chestnut neck. "I know," she said. "It's scary having a baby, but Drew will take care of you when the time comes."

Pavlova nickered, and Callie laughed softly. "You'll be fine without me. You'll be so busy with your new foal you won't even notice I'm gone." The mare turned toward her and nuzzled her gently. Callie wrapped her arms around the velvety brown neck and squeezed.

"I'll miss you, too," she whispered, dropping a kiss on Pavlova's broad nose. As she left the barn, she noticed the wrought-iron latch on the door was loose. She'd have to remember to have Nate fix it. And one of the doors to the half baths was sticking and could use planing. She swallowed back a lump. It was hard to remember this place wouldn't be her responsibility anymore.

Back in the house, she busied herself in the routine of feeding Hannah. Callie leaned against the counter to watch the spaniel as she ate. When finished, Hannah gave her bowl a finishing swipe with her tongue just to make sure no morsel remained.

Hannah might have slimmed down, Callie thought, but the dog would always live to eat, not eat to live. She stooped and gave the dog a hug and in return received a hearty wet kiss on her cheek from Hannah. Callie laughed even as she choked up again. *Oh, she would so miss this place.*

Wandering through the rooms, closing up the house, Callie realized she had been dreading this moment all day, for now was the time when she must say goodbye to her inn. As she did so, she wanted to remember every tint and hue and shade of its rooms, every texture, every accent she'd so lovingly added over the past two months. She wanted to memorize, indelibly imprint each detail on her heart. Such memories would have to sustain her many a lonely day and night without Iowa, and without Drew.

Stopping outside the west bedroom, she turned the knob and pushed the door open.

It had been done in pale blues and greens, her favorite colors. The enormous walnut armoire nearly covered one wall, yet it didn't dominate the high-ceilinged room. She ran her hand one last time over its dark, smooth surface. She had noticed a gentle desperation in her actions the last few days: a constant need to touch familiar things and people dear to her, open attempts to memorize details.

This had been her parents' bedroom. Their belongings had been moved downstairs to the rooms that Maura would occupy until they returned to Iowa. It would be different for them, like coming back to a whole different home. She hoped they'd like what she'd done. In her heart, she knew they would.

She turned away from the armoire. So her mission here was done now. She lay down on the wide bed, feeling utterly worn out and weary. *I haven't even left and already I'm mourning.*

Exhausted, she drifted into dreamless sleep.

Callie woke suddenly in the darkened room when a branch struck the window and scraped across the side of the house. She rose and crossed silently to the window, her arms clasped tightly around her ribs. Lightning lit the southwestern skies and revealed the approaching thunderheads. Her sleepiness vanished, and that old apprehension dug in. It seemed the Iowa weather meant to see her off with a bang.

She felt her way down the hall, calling to Hannah as she moved uncertainly in the dark. She tried to quell the agitation that churned in her abdomen as a muffled crack of thunder sounded in the distance.

Callie stopped briefly to feel inside the linen closet and pull an old quilt from the shelf before descending the stairs. Her focus riveted on a large flashlight in the kitchen, charging in its stand on the counter. Feeling her way, she grabbed the flashlight and started toward the cellar stairs when she glanced out the window over the sink. A brilliant flash of lightning illuminated the landscape for brief seconds. She stopped mid-movement, her breath caught in her throat.

The barn door was open.

Callie moved swiftly to the back door and thrust it open, and a wind gust nearly whipped it out of her hand. Another brilliant bolt etched her surroundings in eerie light, revealing dark, grim thunderheads hovering over the fields like great scavenging beasts. Her eyes had not deceived her. The door gaped open.

"Pav!" she screamed. She gripped the rail of the porch to hold herself upright. She couldn't see a thing. The wind seemed to whip away even her own thoughts, and she struggled against the harsh gusts, unprepared and momentarily incapacitated.

With a jolt, Callie realized she'd be swept away if she didn't retreat immediately. She managed to get back into the house and pull the door shut behind her. With the latch loose, the wind must have blown the barn door open.

Pressing her face against the glass, she tried to see the barn, now a dim shadow in the night. Was Pavlova still in there? The mare usually stayed in her stall these days, so Callie had taken to leaving it unlatched. Pavlova was probably there now, safe in a corner, and all Callie had to do now was run out and secure the barn door. A flash, then a warning rumble came up through the floor, through her feet and legs, into her chest.

All? she derided herself.

She stood tensely, her eyes fixed on the yard, waiting for the next bolt of lightning. When it came, she gave a strangled cry. Very clearly, she had seen Pavlova. In the paddock the mare reared, forelegs raking the air wildly.

She was out there. *Oh, my poor Pav.*

Callie turned back into the kitchen, frantically glancing about for a solution. Pavlova would hurt herself and the foal if not coaxed back into the barn.

She hesitated only a split second, then crossed to the telephone and jerked the receiver from its cradle. She impatiently dialed Nate's number before realizing the line was dead.

"Damn!" she swore. Knocking a chair over in her haste to return to the back door, she stared hard into the gloom, not even risking a blink, her sweating palms pressed to the glass. After a moment, lightning flashed and she glimpsed Pavlova. But in less than a second, the mare was again engulfed in the ferocious darkness.

Callie's heart thundered nearly at the pitch of the storm, and she had to grip the doorjamb to steady herself. Even if she could reach the mare, it would take a superhuman effort to control her. *Go back in the barn, Pav. Please.* A torch of lightning ripped across the sky, and she saw the mare combating the wind. It was no use. Pavlova was hysterically frightened. Callie could achieve nothing by forging into the storm after the mare. Nothing, and perhaps she would get herself hurt in the process. In her frenzy, the horse would lash out blindly, and those hooves could wound deeply.

Yet she knew she must help Pavlova, if the mare were to live.

She fought the paralyzing fear rising in her throat. Terrifying details of being caught in that violent storm years ago invaded her mind in a vivid onslaught—a maelstrom of confusion and helplessness against an unstoppable force. The memory filled her chest and choked her, chased her like demons after a wandering soul.

Precious moments ticked by as Callie relived her terror, indecision now overrunning and compounding the recollection. Memories of the last time she'd relived this crippling panic flooded her consciousness. Then, Drew had comforted and held her.

Drew. Drew, I need you. The prayer for help died in her throat. She was alone, on her own. But what should she do? What *could* she do? Pavlova, her beautiful Pavlova and her precious unborn foal, were caught in that storm, fighting a losing battle.

Shaking to her marrow, bone cold, Callie closed her eyes as her past terror bored into her mind with dark, menacing eyes. *Stop, I need to think!* But an awful grip clamped over her. Pavlova could die out there... It can't be that bad... *Oh, yes it is* ... The terrible fear... fear for Pavlova.

Callie opened her eyes, wrenched open the door, and plunged into the storm.

Chapter Twelve

Dust and dirt clogged her eyes and nostrils and grit coated her tongue as Callie shouted to the mare. Knocked to her knees as the wind buffeted her slight form, she struggled to her feet, choking as the wind brutally drove her cries back down her throat. Lightning tore out of the sky in frantic, terrifying tentacles, illuminating the massive blue black thunderheads bearing down on her. Still, she pressed on.

Callie stopped only once to catch her breath, flattening herself against the barn before slipping inside to grab a bridle and halter. Amazingly, Hannah had followed her there, and Callie commanded the dog to stay before she staggered back into the storm, her tears washing away some of the dirt blinding her eyes.

"Pavlova!" she screamed and spun around when she felt rather than heard the pounding of hysterical hooves near her. "Pavlova!"

Callie held her arm over her eyes as a shield against the gale. The mare was a dark, lurching shadow, the whites of her eyes starkly visible, moving in wide arcs as the horse tossed her head wildly. Callie took a step, then stumbled back to avoid being trampled.

Again and again, she tried to approach the mare, at one point even managing to get near enough to slip the bridle over one ear. But another streak of lightning caused Pavlova to rear against the restriction, lifting Callie off her feet. She crashed to the ground as the mare galloped off into the gloom.

Callie dragged herself to her feet, stifling the sobs of defeat that rose in her throat, but ready to try again. Out of the corner of her eye she caught a movement, and a streak of elemental fear tore through her chest before she felt a hard pressure on her arm.

"Drew!"

He was beside her, grabbing her other arm as he shouted words the wind whipped away. She shook her head mutely and he bent closer. Without hearing his actual words, she understood what he wanted. He moved to place himself on the other side of Pavlova, and together they tried to steer the horse toward the barn. Callie spread her arms as he did and sidestepped, trying to aim Pavlova's frenzied movements in the proper direction, but with the storm closing in Callie feared only a miracle would save them all.

Hoarse from screaming and the grit collected in her throat, she cried the mare's name over and over, her arms leaden extensions of her shoulders as they flailed, partially to keep her upright, partially to direct Pavlova's movement.

Finally, unbelievably, they managed to head off the mare as she pivoted this way and that. Inch by inch, the two of them guided Pavlova's zigzagging path toward the barn. When close enough that the structure blocked some of the wind, the horse calmed a little and Drew slipped the bridle over Pavlova's head and led her into the barn.

"Down, Hannah," he said curtly as he guided the horse to a corner of the barn. Pavlova had become suddenly docile and followed with her head down. Callie watched Hannah trail them at a safe distance, then pulled the barn door shut. The wind still raged with deafening force outside, but she barely heard it. Her ears were ringing, and she took a moment to rub the grime from her eyes as she fought to catch her breath.

Callie reached for a switch. With relief, she saw the bare light bulb overhead come on, dimly defining the interior of the barn. She found a board and ran it through the wrought-iron handle where it braced the door shut. Then she walked over to where Drew stood calming the mare in low tones. He turned at her approach.

"Just what did you think you were doing?" he demanded, his blue eyes glittering, black hair wind tossed and wild. She'd seen that look before, as he'd bent over Rusty.

"I had to save her, Drew," she said between gasps of breath. "I had to."

"You could have been killed! In one sudden turn, she'd have trampled you under her and neither of you would've even known it."

"I couldn't just let her die in this storm!" Callie shouted back, her terror of a moment ago making her quick to anger. "What was I supposed to do?"

"You could have given me a call!"

"And listen to you scold me like a child? No thanks!" She pushed her tangled hair out of her face with an indignant gesture. "And besides, the phones are dead. Even without them you seem to have your own ideas about when little Callie Farrell needs your help, or you wouldn't be here!"

"Damn right you need my help. Somehow I got the impression you were terrified of storms!" he said angrily, his eyes sparking.

"I am! But I'm not going to let something I love die because of it!"

They stood staring at each other, their breathing ragged and short. Drew's jaw clenched and unclenched furiously, his fear for her stark on his face. Finally he said, "Look, let's talk about this later. Right now, Pavlova's the one who needs our help."

Callie took a step forward. "Is she going into labor?"

He circled around the mare, who now stood completely still. His hands were prodding but gentle as he examined her. "I'm afraid so."

"What do you want me to do?" she asked, the flaring tempers of a moment ago forgotten. "I cleaned and scrubbed her stall a few days ago. Shouldn't she be in there?"

"Not tonight." Drew rolled up the sleeves of his shirt and set his hands on his hips, looking around him. "That storm has all the makings of a tornado. If we've got to be in here— which isn't the safest place in the world during a twister— then the southwest corner is the best location. Here." He strode to the front of the barn where a large, old worktable stood with tools, a few empty pots and gardening paraphernalia scattered upon it. With a fluid motion, Drew lifted the side and tipped it. Everything slid to the floor with a clatter. "Help me drag this over to the corner. It'll be a little cramped under there, but it's better than no protection at all."

When the table was standing in place, Drew spread an old blanket under it. "I hope you're not attached to this thing," he remarked to Callie. He coaxed the mare over to lie on the blanket, with her head lying under the table.

"Get under there and keep Pavlova calm," he instructed. "I'm going to get some things from the Bronco."

Callie scrambled under the table and settled the mare's head in her lap as Hannah sank down next to her. She tried to ignore the howling gales shaking the rafters but despite the trickle of perspiration running down her spine goose bumps rose in waves across her arms, neck and scalp.

Above, the pitiful bulb flared, ebbed, then was snuffed.

Stay calm, she told herself. The courage that had spurred her thus far waned as the storm grew in intensity. *Pavlova needs you. Drew needs you.*

With effort she made her voice serene and soothing as she stroked the horse's broad neck.

Relief swelled in her tight chest when Drew returned. He had his medical kit, the flashlight and clean towels from the house.

"How is she?" he asked.

"She seems fine." He positioned the flashlight and then went to Pavlova's stall and brought back what was left of her water. Taking a bar of soap from the medical kit, he washed his hands and forearms up to the elbows. When he had rinsed and dried on one of the towels, he knelt to examine Pavlova.

The mare's breathing had become quick and rapid. She arched her back, chest expanding, and Callie saw movements under the rock-hard muscles of her abdomen. She smoothed the mare's mane, talking to her comfortingly as Drew concentrated on doing his job.

"Good," he said, straightening and wiping his hands on the towel. "I can see some presentation and her water just broke." He looked up at Callie and nodded. "She's doing fine. Not too long now."

He settled back against one of the legs of the table and closed his eyes. It had started to rain and blasts of bullet-hard drops buffeted the sides of the barn. The storm was nearly on them now, and thunder exploded with earthshaking force.

Callie shivered. "It's really bad out, isn't it, Drew?"

He nodded. "I eased the Bronco into the ditch to keep it from getting bashed into by flying debris. And I cracked open a few windows in the house, just in case."

She knew why he'd done that. A tornado, if close enough, could produce low-pressure suction, causing every window in a house to explode outward.

"You don't have to stay here," Drew said suddenly. His wrists were propped on his knees, and his black brows shadowed his eyes in the dimness. "I can get you and Hannah back to the house. You'll be safer in the cellar than here."

She hesitated for just a moment, then shook her head. "I won't leave you and Pav. You need me."

"We'll survive, Callie—if the storm doesn't blow down the barn. It could happen, and I'd rather you were in the most sheltered place available." He ran a hand through his hair. "There's no sense in both of us risking our lives. I don't want to alarm you, Callie, but it could come to that."

Without answering, Callie bent her head and continued to speak softly to Pavlova, telling the mare how brave and beautiful she was, but her mind churned with almost as much turbulence as the air outside.

Yes, they were virtually helpless, the only resources at their command those which enabled them to protect themselves and very little else. Callie thought of Nate and his half-grown crops, defenseless to such an assault. There were all the other farmers' crops, the homes of the people in town, their businesses. Drew's clinic. She closed her eyes and prayed that the storm was not as terrible as it sounded, that those she loved would survive it unscathed. And that those who needed her could count on her.

"I can't leave you," she said. "I won't."

She avoided his eyes, afraid that by meeting them she might be forced into another struggle of wills with him. But Drew said nothing, and Callie lost herself momentarily in the task of soothing the mare. Her thoughts were jerked back by Drew's muttered curse. He was kneeling over Pavlova again.

"What is it, Drew?"

"I'm not sure." He dipped into the medical kit again and opened a tube of antiseptic lubricant. He stripped off his shirt and began to rub the lubricant into his hand and up his arm. "We should be seeing a more definite presentation by now. Keep talking to her," he commanded and bent to examine the mare.

A few minutes later he cursed again and withdrew his arm. He sat back and met Callie's eyes across the mare's expanse. "The foal's in a posterior presentation. Completely turned around. This isn't going to be as smooth as I'd hoped, Callie. If the cord becomes compressed between the foal's chest and Pavlova's pelvic girdle, we . . . we could lose them."

"Oh, Drew, no!"

His blue gaze leveled on her. "We've got a critical window of time in which to act. We're going to have to put some traction on the little guy—if we don't get him out of there quickly, he'll suffocate. Can I depend on you?"

She didn't hesitate. "What do you want me to do?"

"Stay there for now, but be ready to help when I say so."

Pavlova began to thrash around as Drew helped with her delivery. Callie held the horse's head firmly, talking to the mare more loudly now, but still in comforting tones. She could barely hear her own thoughts; the roar outside sounded like a freight train bearing down at full speed. The sides and roof of the barn shook, peppered with bracken and chunks of things torn loose by the storm.

Time passed slowly, an eternity, much too long for a small foal to survive without air. *I can't lose them, not now,* she thought desperately. One mare, a tiny foal—they didn't deserve to die. But death knew no justice. *Death takes the beings we love without cause. It doesn't listen to arguments.* She closed her eyes, as if to shut out her own thoughts. Behind her eyelids burned the image of Rusty, and Drew's face.

No! She opened her eyes. They'd fight every step of the way. They had to.

She glanced at Drew. A dry sob of helpless empathy escaped her throat as she watched his face contort with effort, perspiration glistening and dripping from his straining muscles.

"Push, Pav," she pleaded. "Oh, push, girl."

The noise of the storm escalated with the tension in the barn, and she clamped her lips tight against the terror that clambered upward, digging into the walls of her chest. It seemed unbelievable that the roof hadn't come crashing down on them all. Hannah braced tensely against her, and the dog whimpered.

"Now, Callie!" Drew directed suddenly through clenched teeth, and she scrambled from beneath the weight of Pavlova's heavy head to his side. "Grab the other leg, just above the fetlock. And *pull!*"

Her hands circled the slick limb, and she dug in her heels, tugging with all her might, shoulder to shoulder with Drew. Her head roared as the turbulence outdoors reached an even more violent pitch. Everything about them—Drew, Pavlova, Hannah, even the barn—strained against heaven-knew-what demonic force. Callie gave a moan of frustrated effort but never loosened her grip on the foal's leg. *Don't die!*

For several moments they made no progress, but then suddenly she felt some slack, then more—and the foal lay on the towels at their feet, wet and disturbingly limp.

"Quickly, Callie," Drew sprang to the foal's head and began clearing its nostrils and mouth of fluid, "grab a towel and rub him—*hard!*"

Callie rubbed vigorously, willing her strength and life into the little creature on the floor. "Come on, fella," she urged, her voice cracking. "Come on. Don't die on us."

Drew shook the colt forcefully and it began to struggle with spasmodic gasps and snorts. Its nose, pointing skyward, pitched to and fro, seeking, seeking. Callie's own breath was strangled. Finally the little chest contracted and then miraculously expanded, and the foal filled its lungs with air.

He lay on his side for a few moments, sputtering the remaining fluid from his nostrils. He strove to sit upright, hind legs drawn under him and forelegs outstretched. Precariously balanced, he shook his head so energetically he nearly unseated himself and looked around with pink, bleary eyes. Then he neighed, a precious trilling down the scale that made both Callie and Drew smile as they knelt in the hay beside him, hot, tired and relieved.

"Look at them," she said in a clogged voice as Pavlova struggled to sit up and lick the foal. Callie turned to the man beside her. "*This* is why you became a veterinarian," she

said. "Moments like these, where you made a difference."
She smiled her approbation, her heart filling for his accomplishment. His affirmation. This was *his* dream, and she thanked God that she'd been allowed to share it with him. And if he hadn't been here—

"Thank you, Drew. From Pavlova and me. We would never have brought him into this world safely without you."

"Without us, Callie," Drew murmured, his expert gaze still examining the foal. "I couldn't have done it alone."

"I guess I do need you," she murmured by way of apology, then realizing how personal her words sounded, added, "for miracles and such."

"I need you as much as you need me." He searched her face. "I care about you, Callie, very much. You know that, don't you?"

"I know." She had never contended that fact.

Suddenly she found herself exhausted by the physical and emotional effort of the last few hours, and very close to tears. Blindly, needing human contact, her hand sought his in the prickly hay and his fingers clasped hers warmly. With her other hand she stroked the foal rhythmically, barely aware she did so.

"What shall we name him?" she asked, wanting to keep this moment forever in her heart.

Drew swabbed the back of his neck with one of the clean towels. "I don't know. How about Cyclone?"

She smiled shakily. "Cyclone? This sweet baby?" She thought a moment, studying the small brown creature making valiant efforts to stand and failing miserably. "I'll call him Stormy."

"As Sancho's son, I've no doubt he'll live up to the name."

No doubt he will, Callie thought, and once again tears swam in her eyes. He'd be so big when she came back next year. Hardly a colt anymore.

"Oh, Drew, how can I leave?" she cried suddenly.

"I don't know," he said softly. "How can you?"

She withdrew her hand from his and clenched it in her lap. "But I have to go. I can't stay, not—" She plunged her face into her hands. *Not loving you as I do, when you don't love me the same way.*

She felt Drew's arm go around her, felt his cheek against her hair. "Why couldn't you stay, Callie? What would it take to make you stay?"

Callie pushed away from him and stood. She made her tear-drenched gaze take in the scene before her: Hannah, chin on her paws as brown eyes avidly watched the mare with her new foal; Pavlova, her coat glistening like polished mahogany, nosing her newborn, making her own assessment of his health; the foal, nuzzling his mother's flank, instinctively seeking nourishment.

And Drew, sitting in the golden hay, forearms propped on his bent knees as he waited for her answer.

What would it take? The impossible. Drew loving her, as she so loved him.

"A miracle," Callie whispered. "It would take a miracle."

Drew met her gaze steadily before his own fell away. He shook his head. "I just used up my quota of miracles for the month, I'm afraid. If this didn't do it, I don't know what will." He rolled to his feet, reaching for his shirt. "It'll be an hour or so before Pavlova expels the afterbirth. You look beat. We could both use a shower and a cup of coffee."

He cocked his head to one side and listened. For the first time, Callie noticed how very quiet it had become in the barn. The storm had passed. Only pattering rain remained. "Sounds like things have calmed down out there," he said. "We'd better have a look."

He pulled open the barn door and Callie followed him outside. She was surprised to see a predawn haze breaking dimly over the horizon. But the pale, dull light revealed devastation.

The chicken coop was gone. Branches from trees and pieces of boards littered the yard. The small maple in the paddock lay uprooted by the gale-force winds. Nearly every shingle on the garage had been stripped off. Then, as Callie and Drew walked nearer, they saw the real damage.

It was gone. Gone. The inn was rubble. It didn't seem possible, but as they had sat just fifty yards away, a tornado had cut a knife-sharp gash through the countryside, and her inn had been in its path.

Unrecognizable debris. There was no question of salvaging anything. Callie stood and stared at the destruction that barely three hours had wreaked on her and what she loved. In a daze, she turned to Drew, shock creeping outward from her stunned core.

"Callie..." he began, but she was already running toward the spot where had last stood the front door.

She stopped short of that site, as if by some unseen barrier—because there was no front door, no porch, nothing. She fought for control, the ability to make sense of this catastrophe, but all her defenses had already been marshaled to protect her from the pain of absolute despair filling her. Her world had been ripped from its axis, creating a void—a terrible, terrible void that threatened to cave in on itself.

She pressed her hands against her head, fingers creeping upward through her hair, as if to contain her pain. But it wouldn't be contained. Her inn was gone, a stark reality nothing would change. Nothing would help. Nothing, except—

Callie turned. Drew stood but a few feet away, his own hands fisted against his sides. His face revealed a torment rivaling hers. Everything she felt at that moment—all the pain, the grief, the loss and more—were all reflected in his deep blue eyes.

"I'm sorry, Callie," he murmured. "Sweetheart, I'm so, so sorry."

She felt it crumple then, that terrible emptiness.

Callie stumbled forward, blinded by tears, her hand out in appeal. "Drew..."

He stepped toward her, caught her in his arms and held her against him as she sobbed brokenly. He smoothed her dark hair with his hand and rocked her gently.

"That's right, hold on to me. I'm here. I'll help you, whatever it takes."

"It's gone, Drew." She wrapped her arms around him, her anchor, the only force strong enough to pull her back from the gulf that threatened to suck her in. Pressing her face into the curve of his neck, she tried to move closer, to draw on the strength she so needed from him at this moment. "Mom and Dad's home— Oh, Drew, what will I tell them?"

"Shh. They'll be fine as long as they know you are." He brushed back her hair with unbelievable tenderness. "And though it's small consolation right now, I'm sure they've got good insurance."

"But I've failed them!" she cried, wild with despair.

"Ah, no, honey, you haven't failed anyone. You can't be responsible for the storm. It'll be all right. We'll think of something, together."

"How? What will I do?" The shock deepened, the despair thickened, a congestion that cut off her air and made her gasp in ineffective, powerless breaths. *"Why did this happen?"*

"I don't know." Drew's voice was nearly as anguished as her own. "But you're not alone, Callie." With sudden emotion, he crushed her to him, as if he too, could not get close enough. "Come back to Iowa," he said. "Come back to me, and I promise we'll think of something together."

He tugged her away from him and put his hands on either side of her face, thumbs caressing her damp cheekbones as he stared intently into her eyes. "You can't go back to California. I'm afraid if you do, you'll never come back." His eyes burned into her, begging her to return to sanity. "I don't know what we'll do yet, but you must come back to me, Callie."

She blinked and her mind cleared infinitesimally. What was he saying? It didn't seem . . .

The events of the last two months flooded her consciousness: Drew's demand that she promise to hold onto her dreams; his protectiveness and pride as he shielded her from his own disappointments and setbacks; his efforts to show her, aside from himself, what Iowa had to offer her. And his struggle to maintain his distance, lest he influence her against her better judgment and her own pursuit of happiness. Through all of these experiences, she had always known that he cared, perhaps as a brother or a friend, but that he cared.

She gazed up at him and saw with a newly acquired perception what this man really felt for her. In his eyes she saw love, as she had seen it before, but now she saw the pain of that love, in a way the fear of it. But still, above all, a selfless and indefatigable love.

Callie pulled away and found she could stand on her own. She turned back to the rubble, the ruination of a dream. "But what would I do, if I came back?"

Drew offered no answer for a moment, then said, "There's the referral network, and helping people set up inns."

She shook her head. "I could, but... it's not enough."

Another pause. "You could help your parents rebuild— another inn. They need to come back to something."

"Yes, we could rebuild," she said slowly. "Another inn. It won't be the same, but—" Tears of relief came to her eyes. "Mom and Dad would never have to see this, then, never have to have their hearts broken this way." But again she shook her head. "This is their home, not mine."

"There's mine." He seemed to be grasping at straws now. "Use my home for your inn... And if that's not enough, then you can help me run the clinic."

She closed her eyes, remembering how she'd stood in Drew's bedroom and wondered if he thought of Maura as he worked there. *Offering his house and himself as proof of his love. Needing nothing more.* Could he possibly have been thinking of someone else?

Then Callie heard the words she'd so longed to hear, the only words that could make a difference, as if Drew had read her mind:

"I love you, Callie. Come back to me."

She faced him. His shirt stuck in wet patches to his chest, and his damp hair curled over his brow. Beads of the drizzling rain clung to his forehead and in his hopelessly disheveled black hair. The strain of the past several hours had taken their toll. His eyes were shadowed with weariness and a day-old beard obscured the lean lines of his face.

He looked utterly wonderful, and she had never loved him more.

"I could come back, do all those things," she said softly. "But it's not enough, Drew. That would never be enough."

He tensed, every muscle in him, it seemed, striving to hold back argument, but knowing he had no other.

"If I'm to come back to Iowa," Callie said, "all I want is you."

His eyes widened. His throat worked for a moment, then he asked, "And just what do you mean, Callie Farrell, when you say you want me?"

She recognized the words, remembered a time when a seventeen-year-old girl had not known how to express herself, had not been up to the love of this man. Well, she'd grown up a lot since then. No, no longer was she "sweet" on him. She'd gone far beyond that point.

Callie took the steps that separated them and put her arms around his neck. "Dear Drew," she whispered. "I love you, I need you. I want to live with you, love with you, suffer what you suffer, forever and ever."

The restraint he had maintained crumbled, and Drew gathered Callie to him with a groan. "God, Callie, don't ever leave me again," he murmured into her hair.

"Then don't send me away," she said.

His hand slid through her glossy hair and Drew kissed the crown of her head with quiet passion. "I would never have, you know, if I'd known you'd stay away."

Callie lifted her head and smiled at him. She had needed to hear that. "It's behind us now."

He smiled back, then became serious. "Callie, I grieve inside for you and your inn. I'd give anything, anything not to have had that happen. But now we can fulfill your dreams together. Now they can be mine, too."

"All I've dreamed of for ages is being with you."

He smiled. "What a coincidence. I've had the same dream. You in my heart and home forever."

At his words, her love for him welled up within her and spilled over. How, out of the destruction and ruination of this dream, had she found her heart's desire?

"It's a miracle," she said against his lips before taking them to her own. And wrapped within his arms, Callie felt at last that she was home.

*   *   *   *   *

If you enjoyed Callie's story, look out for brother Nate's romance in The Farmer Takes A Wife *Silhouette Romance #992. It will be available in February 1994! Happy Reading!*

HE'S MORE THAN A MAN, HE'S ONE OF OUR

HELP WANTED: DADDY
Carolyn Monroe

Newspaperman Boone Shelton thought he'd seen everything—until a couple of enterprising kids placed a classified ad to find a new husband for their unsuspecting mom. Then Boone found out "mom" was none other than his childhood dream girl, Nixie Cordaire Thomas! The children were ready to consider all applicants—especially fun-loving Boone. Now if he could just prove to Nixie he was the best man for the job....

Available in November from Silhouette Romance.

Fall in love with our **Fabulous Fathers!**

Silhouette
R O M A N C E™

Take 4 bestselling love stories FREE

Plus get a FREE surprise gift!

Special Limited-time Offer

Mail to Silhouette Reader Service®

P.O. Box 609
Fort Erie, Ontario
L2A 5X3

YES! Please send me 4 free Silhouette Romance® novels and my free surprise gift. Then send me 6 brand-new novels every month, which I will receive months before they appear in bookstores. Bill me at the low price of $2.25 each plus 25¢ delivery and GST*. That's the complete price and—compared to the cover prices of $2.75 each—quite a bargain! I understand that accepting the books and gift places me under no obligation ever to buy any books. I can always return a shipment and cancel at any time. Even if I never buy another book from Silhouette, the 4 free books and the surprise gift are mine to keep forever.

315 BPA AJJF

Name	(PLEASE PRINT)	
Address		Apt. No.
City	Province	Postal Code

This offer is limited to one order per household and not valid to present Silhouette Romance® subscribers.
*Terms and prices are subject to change without notice.
Canadian residents will be charged applicable provincial taxes and GST.

Silhouette Books has done it again!

Opening night in October has never been as exciting! Come watch as the curtain rises and romance flourishes when the stars of tomorrow make their debuts today!

Revel in Jodi O'Donnell's STILL SWEET ON HIM—
Silhouette Romance #969
...as Callie Farrell's renovation of the family homestead leads her straight into the arms of teenage crush Drew Barnett!

Tingle with Carol Devine's BEAUTY AND THE BEASTMASTER—
Silhouette Desire #816
...as legal eagle Amanda Tarkington is carried off by wrestler Bram Masterson!

Thrill to Elyn Day's A BED OF ROSES—
Silhouette Special Edition #846
...as Dana Whitaker's body and soul are healed by sexy physical therapist Michael Gordon!

Believe when Kylie Brant's McLAIN'S LAW —
Silhouette Intimate Moments #528
...takes you into detective Connor McLain's life as he falls for psychic—and suspect—Michele Easton!

Catch the classics of tomorrow—*premiering* today—
only from ❤️ *Silhouette*

And now for something completely different from Silhouette....

SPELLBOUND
R O M A N C E

Every once in a while, Silhouette brings you a book that is truly unique and innovative, taking you into the world of paranormal happenings. And now these stories will carry our special "Spellbound" flash, letting you know that you're in for a truly exciting reading experience!

In October, look for *McLain's Law* (IM #528) by Kylie Brant

Lieutenant Detective Connor McLain believes only in what he can see—until Michele Easton's haunting visions help him solve a case...and her love opens his heart!

McLain's Law is also the Intimate Moments "Premiere" title, introducing you to a debut author, sure to be the star of tomorrow!

Available in October...only from Silhouette Intimate Moments

SILHOUETTE.... Where Passion Lives

Don't miss these Silhouette favorites by some of our most popular authors!
And now, you can receive a discount by ordering two or more titles!

Silhouette Desire®

#05751	THE MAN WITH THE MIDNIGHT EYES BJ James	$2.89	☐
#05763	THE COWBOY Cait London	$2.89	☐
#05774	TENNESSEE WALTZ Jackie Merritt	$2.89	☐
#05779	THE RANCHER AND THE RUNAWAY BRIDE Joan Johnston	$2.89	☐

Silhouette Intimate Moments®

#07417	WOLF AND THE ANGEL Kathleen Creighton	$3.29	☐
#07480	DIAMOND WILLOW Kathleen Eagle	$3.39	☐
#07486	MEMORIES OF LAURA Marilyn Pappano	$3.39	☐
#07493	QUINN EISLEY'S WAR Patricia Gardner Evans	$3.39	☐

Silhouette Shadows®

#27003	STRANGER IN THE MIST Lee Karr	$3.50	☐
#27007	FLASHBACK Terri Herrington	$3.50	☐
#27009	BREAK THE NIGHT Anne Stuart	$3.50	☐
#27012	DARK ENCHANTMENT Jane Toombs	$3.50	☐

Silhouette Special Edition®

#09754	THERE AND NOW Linda Lael Miller	$3.39	☐
#09770	FATHER: UNKNOWN Andrea Edwards	$3.39	☐
#09791	THE CAT THAT LIVED ON PARK AVENUE Tracy Sinclair	$3.39	☐
#09811	HE'S THE RICH BOY Lisa Jackson	$3.39	☐

Silhouette Romance®

#08893	LETTERS FROM HOME Toni Collins	$2.69	☐
#08915	NEW YEAR'S BABY Stella Bagwell	$2.69	☐
#08927	THE PURSUIT OF HAPPINESS Anne Peters	$2.69	☐
#08952	INSTANT FATHER Lucy Gordon	$2.75	☐

	AMOUNT	$ _____
DEDUCT:	**10% DISCOUNT FOR 2+ BOOKS**	$ _____
	POSTAGE & HANDLING	$ _____
	($1.00 for one book, 50¢ for each additional)	
	APPLICABLE TAXES*	$ _____
	TOTAL PAYABLE	$ _____
	(check or money order—please do not send cash)	

To order, complete this form and send it, along with a check or money order for the total above, payable to Silhouette Books, to: *In the U.S.*: 3010 Walden Avenue, P.O. Box 9077, Buffalo, NY 14269-9077; *In Canada*: P.O. Box 636, Fort Erie, Ontario, L2A 5X3.

Name: _____

Address: _____ City: _____

State/Prov.: _____ Zip/Postal Code: _____

*New York residents remit applicable sales taxes.
Canadian residents remit applicable GST and provincial taxes.

SBACK-OD

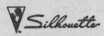